Th

Ten Million Steps Across Canada

Henry "Hank" Gallant

The Walk

Ten Million Steps Across Canada

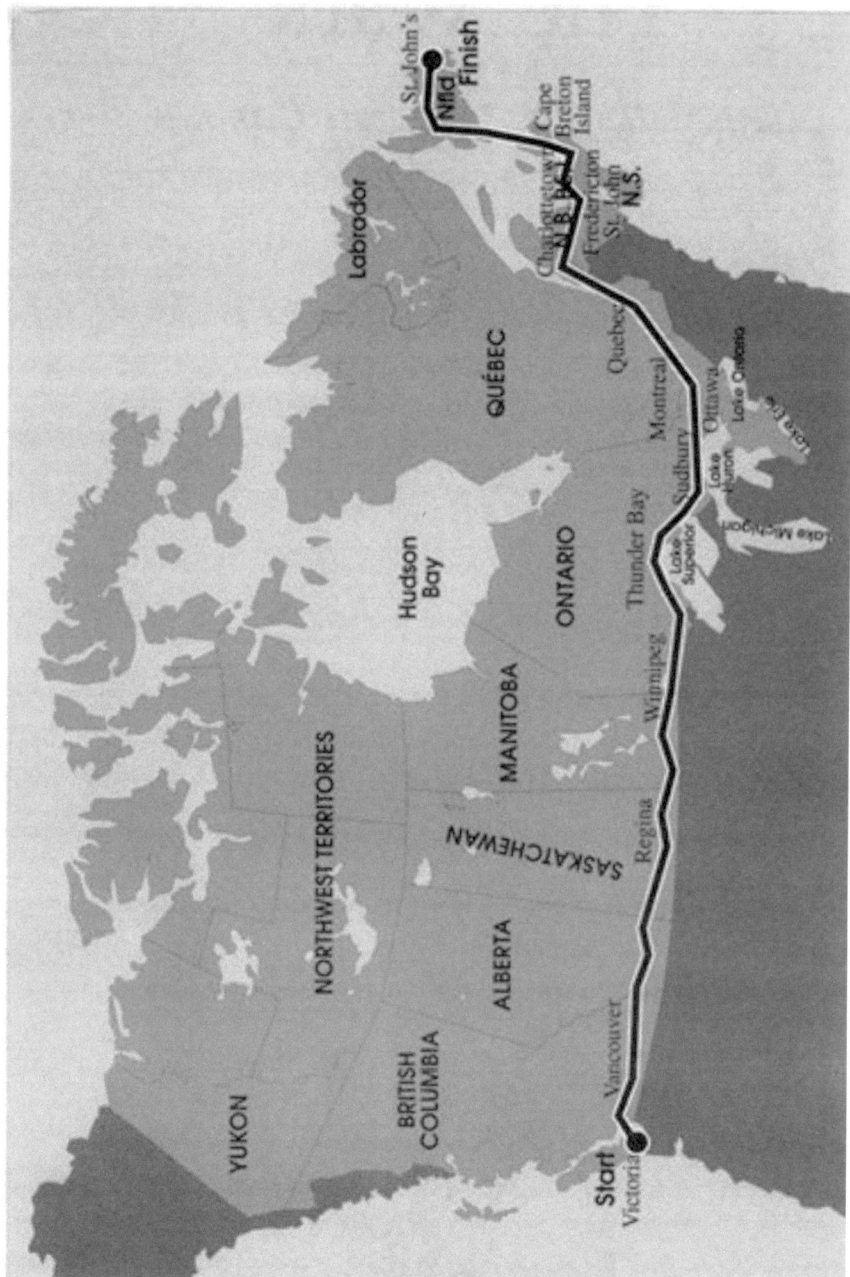

Acknowledgement

Firstly, I thank God for giving me the determination and a strong-willed mind to never give up on the walk, also to my mom, Veronica, who prayed and supported me through this challenge.

Secondly, the manuscript, which was completed in 1971 with the help of my wife and friend Doloris. To my youngest son Jonathan who participated in a School Heritage project, birthed the book title. Also, my friend Edward FitzGerald who encouraged and helped me in this endeavor.

Finally, the assistance from the 1999 Tignish Bicentennial Committee in having this book "The Walk – Ten Million Steps Across Canada" published.

To the Canadian people who encouraged and supported me on my centennial project, and to those who were not so helpful; my victory was to share with you some moments, thoughts and adventures.

- *Henry (Hank) Gallant*

During my walk, my observations, thoughts, and feelings were journaled daily while using English and French words, like A painter uses A brush… except without A camera, A phone or A watch. At an early age, my country school teacher taught me how to B observant with words by describing people, places and things. The Who, Why and Where are words painted in my book "The Walk: Ten Million Steps Across Canada"

Table of Contents

ACKNOWLEDGEMENT ii

CHAPTER 1 TO HOPE AND BEYOND.…….................................. 1

CHAPTER 2 TRIALS AND TRIBULATIONS 16

CHAPTER 3 MOUNTAINS AND MOLEHILLS… 32

CHAPTER 4 CHINOOK PHOBIA…. 46

CHAPTER 5 LA VERENDRYES COUNTRY.................................. 62

CHAPTER 6 THE VERDANT MOULDED LAKES IN THE WOODS............ 77

CHAPTER 7 BUSH AND BLACK FLIES 91

CHAPTER 8 OPERATION DESPERATION.................................100

CHAPTER 9 A JOB OF WORK…. 105

CHAPTER 10 LONESOME HIGHEWAY BLUES…. 114

CHAPTER 11 WE DON'T ALLOW NO GUITAR PLAYING HERE….........124

CHAPTER 12 TO MONTREAL WITH ITCH….. 130

CHAPTER 13 HABITANT HOSPITALITY…. 137

CHAPTER 14 LOVE FABULATION…. 148

CHAPTER 15 BREATHES THERE A MAN….................................158

CHAPTER 16 THE OX LAND KILT….....................................172

CHAPTER 17 THE LAST LEG…. 186

Chapter 1

TO HOPE AND BEYOND.........

Freezing water temperatures calls feet bathing or christening ridiculous my friend, on the last Pacific touch and the beginning of my East-to-Atlantic pack walk. Beyond Mile Zero, Victoria lies; this foggy February sixth morning, 1967, draped with the existing feeling of British ancestral beings. Struggling through this to-work-human-void, I receive my first ray glimpse piercing the morning fog.

"Good luck Hank. Your picture with column will B in our local evening paper. We'll probably hear later of your failure."

"Thanks for nothing."

"Reporting, I get paid."

Swartz Bay terminal ------- thirteen miles. The highway embankment descends to A swale cat-tail pond. Mid-day sun five hands high; hellish hungry. I've prepared a cold corn-beef sandwich. Aaah! What a feeling to B finally jaunting after preparation, training and planning. Like this drake mallard, afraid, wondering ------- will he approach the bank where bread crusts await him?

Pacific talked about weather on this bright sixty-above day warms the holly-padded evergreen bank. Lacing my high hiking boots and struggling the fifty-pound house-pack to my back, I'm bonded to the left highway shoulder-whistling accompaniment with each stride.

Dinner being delayed until mid-afternoon, A double burger and milkshake fits my hunger at A roadside café. I answer a few curious questions concerning the long pack-walk to A group of highway workers. Twenty miles I cover and an hour's wait for the 5 PM ferry. Two dollars and eighty cents; it's A lot for A twenty-four-mile sail on the Hero Strait.

Finally disembarking after dark on Tsawassen dock, I proceed, looking for A camp spot but realizing that it's too damp and cold on this sandy beach following Highway Ten. Two miles further, A garage owner allows me to inhabit his cement platform out back. Rats. Should have picked a field ------ much softer.

February ninth; drenched with the persistent Frazer Valley rains, I enter Chilliwack, forcing the prolonged strides with burning pain from twenty-seven blisters gourmeting both feet, caused by these insulated hiking boots. This variety of footwear shop I've entered displays styles to endurance. I've got to have these bloody ovens changed, burned or traded.

Thirty dollars poorer, I'm clobbering my bandaged feet to the musical raindrop tune. Good-looking boots ------ size eight fifty by nine high, with arch support, are better than these other shoes. A small stream flows through the grove; tall ghostlike figures, winterly, whistling the austere nakedness of winter elms.

It's difficult for a small fire setting after two days of drenched pour, I want tea, ------ preferring hot liquids before sack time in my tent on a wet clodded stream bank seventy miles from Victoria. Smoldering flames have warmed McQuack (my kettle), and I'm hidden peacefully from Highway 4 with spring-like smells, as warm rain awakes.

Been once told by an old foot soldier friend that purifying hardens blistered feet like these cooked stubs, where all plasters and solutions failed – the "body urine". I have to try. A thousand needles drum-pierce my nerves and mind, and lips a silent curse. Lying inside five by seven tent, wrapping both ground sheets (and this is supposed to B good bag), I leave both feet uncovered, drying of urine curing. Partially excited with determined sensitiveness, I pluck the old "Gib" pal. Rain drips from nude elm, streak marking my tent to the sponge gray soil.

"Inge girl, what a languor rotten dream." Better dress and pack in acerbic murky rain. Could it have been possible Inge?

Each step in A million. Oh, tremble those mind-rowed clouds in A security cell, explosion dream to expand the sweat-run pores. So very real; I could not acquaint your benevolent mind with eyes that match, and year will pass.

Reality hunger with effort strive, and two more miles before breakfast of two burgers, hot cakes and milk. Settled digestion is difficult with irregular meals and forced pack walking. Dutch strap

3

tightened, also boots and socks changed, for these lighter shoes are restful.

"Hey, whacha doing fella?"

"Pardon?"

"What's written on your pack?"

I turn. "Read for yourself."

"Centennial-um- Walker no rides please. What's all this rigging fannolia got to do with anything? Whatcha provin?"

"I haven't thought much of my journey that way. I'm wasting time."

Standing drenched from reflected showers, those Coast Mountains piercing to B pierced. As smog damp darkness fall, I'm hopeful afraid of night high-way walking. Both feet numb with blisters, I enter the Hope R.C.M.P. office at 8 PM reluctantly and yet helpful, I'm given a dry juvenile cell bunk.

"Hey wake up there U, it's seven."

"Rats, what a short snooze."

Wireless radios, typewriters and drunk noises exceed description. I should B thankful for a dry spring bunk, wash basin, urine drain cell, and these new pure white woolen socks padding my drying blistered clobbers.

Pack-wrapped guitar triangle forms bulk, as I bid good-morning "tank." and young Constable, Hazy challenge each effort strive, and thundering gorge five hundred feet below, I sit, viewing down on fog-wetted Frazer Valley with both feet naked, consciously soaped in wet snow. Turning, facing slippery skyward mount, I leave a hundred flaunty miles behind. This steady climb reminds me of what's to come and each step carefully placed forcefully on the iced gravel shoulder. A maroon Pontiac pulls to the right of me. The heavy well-dressed occupant emerges.

"How are yah? Modern day Coureur de Bois?"

"Not bad. I'm adopting this highway as my own."

"With news description and location, I knew I'd find U in the Hope Pass. Here's a thermos of hot rum, have A shot."

"Thanks, it'll warm my cold bones."

Seventeen miles, nine hours, and five wet snow inches later, I enter an altitude valley where stubble meadow fields are carved from rocky spruce-laid slopes. A ranch-style house with squatty pole barn is perched on the canyon stream bank that drains upper swale fields. I've rested both feet and eyes only in entering Samallo Guest Lodge. After showering, soft cleansing my body from five perspiring walk-a-days, I enjoy a baked bean supper prepared by our proprietress, Mrs. J.A.B. Clark and the Reverend, her husband.

"These genre paintings are yours Sir?"

"Yes Son, the Almighty has helped in many ways. U notice here, the human survey cut through the forest mountains."

"I've passed that canyon view today, between here and Hope."

Allison Pass. February twelfth, A heavy snowfall storm warning, each stride coaxing the thirty hopeful miles in reaching the summit highway workers camp. Savouring the early morning hotcake breakfast, my sliding effort fall to A crashing halt. I sit on the highway snow cutting, untying my right hiking boot after this last spill. Must have stretched something, it's bad; numb pain, without feeling from the knee down. A throbbing panic seeps my body, chilled sweat drops from forehead. "I've gotta move." I carefully place each boot with this erupting leg, and the pain is bearable ---- helped by a branch cane.

In foggy, soot-still soft silence, my eyes view boulder terrain. The highway winds narrow through A sea valley of lime rock slide. A soul twinge, poignant body, noises the padded stillness, and wet falls the snow. With the covered yester deaths, I leave behind the Hope Princeton rock slide.

Meeting A long hauler, he drones the horn, and only I the turtle shuffles the path upward on account of this heavy storm. Darkness finds me six or more bone-chilled miles from highway camp. I want to rest, sleep. "Rats Hank, keep moving you'll freeze." A submonition surveillance. Whatever evades me to stop, as each movement an effort forcing an exhausted nauseated mind, and doggerel crawling through crutch-deep snow, trying to reach A heavy grove. Arriving under a low branch hanging spruce, I drop with pack. Repulsion mind compels my numb hands to "unbuckle the dutch strap". Snow washing and face slapping may help to keep me from freezing to death. Throbbing pain to my left leg. I languor in trial, breaking under-dry branches for a brisk warming fire, while vivid clattering of teeth hold the lit waxed waterproof match. Hours....years,....seem to transcend in void "rechauffer", as orange flames devours. I add more dry branches, trying to warm my feet by jumping and rubbing both hands. This rotten summit cold has turned my wet clothes to an icy granite wrap, as I sit stiffly tugged in my sleeping bag. Warmth emerges, and energize my veins, worrying, waiting for sponge aurora, determined to maintain the stimulant fire and tea kettle hot.

Daybreak; snow-covered mountain forest and cold has partly dried my clothes with the help of this branch fire that forms icicles from snow-laden spruce, dripping the arousing flames. After strapping my leg with a belt, I crawl to the abandoned highway. Hobbling three miles to an invited breakfast from a plowman. I receive first aid treatment for a double bulbous leg at the highway camp, and then leave with hopeful news of Princetons medical attention, sixty miles ahead. Disciplinary mental practice of never allowing difficult matters, torment infernal mile distance, insults, or food money shortage to ponder my mind. I drag my taped stiff leg with the aid of a crutch-branch, dodging plows that are leading vehicles through this three feet of powdery snow. Afternoon resting, I view the snow-laid peaks, erect rock formation, sculptured, standing against the elements and time, but others assigned to a nihil molehill. I feel the vigorous element challenge after spending last night in that K Ranch hay barn, being ten below with darkness, helped my findings without being spotted.

Paying one-fifty for Falls Café breakfast made up of burgers, hotcake and milk, I leave strapping my physical fifty-pound burden pack. Elated elasticity and stride climbing the stifle traverse highway pass, of five miles, then I rest on Sunday summit twenty-five miles from Princetons Doctor.

Aroused to the road by a brisk chill wind, I notice on the South valley slopes, rows of turmoiled catapult trees erupted once by a fierce wind. Downhill walking a vigorous trial and twice the effort from climbing, as three hands high old sol descends, I am refused by a drilling copper foreman of the heated tool shed; he must have thought I'd steal a jackhammer, if my pack isn't plentiful heavy! Eleven sluggard cascade miles, both body and legs cry rest. Conscience repeating, I will not defeat my soul purpose. Four miles since the last food ration has been consumed and I numbly view Princeton from this two mile hill.

Panic strain ascend from this town, and ineptitude from hotel clerk, even to the distinct blood Doctor has something to prove. I'm not dead sick but disreputed, pleading for Princeton medical attention has wasted a day and one costly hotel room. I've gotta strive for Osoyoos.

Cold gray weathered Okanagan range is sheltering me from the heavy South- West wind. The sign reads East. I laugh and tie carefully life existence thermos parka. Similkameen River follows close but yet

8

far from this carnivorous highway. Elegant unslaughtered pines shade a small ranch home, where I'm invited for tea with chili on toast. The old rancher who has read of Hanks pack walk, watch and wave me to enter.

"Here, have some of this, it'll warm you up."

"Thanks. It's damn cold wind."

"I see you gotta bad leg Son?"

"I believe it's a pulled muscle, couldn't see a doctor in Princeton. Now trying for Osoyoos."

"Maybe I could help. No harm, it won't hurt. I've gotta poultice compress for swellings used on cattle and horses. It once worked on my sprained ankle."

"Sounds good."

"Funny town that Princeton, it used to be friendly. These leaves I collect them in the hills, they're boiled. Now pad and bathe your muscle with its juice, also white liniment. Wrap your sprain with this cloth, tape it loosely, leave it stink for three or four days."

"I'm grateful Sir, thanks. By the way, what type of leaves are they?"

"Not telling, it's an old cure. Good-bye, I hope I could help."

"U did Pete, and I'm thankful."

Twelve beatitudes indulgent walk a days. My smile fits the long peak black ball-cap, while listening to the screaming power lines. In reality, I face a forty high wind, whirling dry dust down Richter Pass. Farewell kind Keremeos nestled on the Similkameen River bank, clouded by sky and gray-brown bald Okanagan Range. Got ten dollars for appearing at Elks Banquet last night; big boost to my grub money, and did my best, even if the mouth harp was strained. "Old blues and me, we get along fine, you see." I presume most of my predicting well-wishers wonder, have I vanished, frozen or lost my challenge.

From this sixteen miles halfway to Osoyoos, I view the rolling hills covered with sage brush, torn bushes and stunned evergreens, as I huddle in shelter of a roadside boulder, making up a cold beef sandwich. Man! It's a raw east wind with snow flurries; I sit contemplating and browsing. A loud motor car breaks the screaming wind-cry silence, and a thousand laughs flow from Northern Cariboo city of Prince George. A Simple Simon Moses, to open and walk the sea-forced straits. It was difficult succumbing to what was printed from the council report, concerning my want of sponsorship. Better, hit the road feet, now that my body is immune to the physical strain. Lonely are the disappointments to cause my greater achievement. Harnessed with obedience to mental endurance, I'll try only for happy moments. Sweet Inge, a few good friends. The second visitor of the day advises me to see a doctor and take that lousy poultice off, and handing me a first aid pack, he's deplored and returns to Oliver in his manure-coated half-ton.

Repining exasperation of fifteen minutes late for the five P.M. "Bureau de Poste" closure; damn those hills, ten hours for thirty-two miles. I take a cheap room with bath to subside my leg pain, aaah! Good old horse doctor.

"I'll have roast chicken, mashed potatoes, soup and milk. Do you have any cream pies?"

"Yes, banana."

"Fine, thanks."

She putters to the kitchen, crushing my smiling countenance to the staunch consort plastic world, leaving the self-challenged grooving Hank. Delicious supper thanks.

Now the soft spring sack time, speak the adventures on each wind-blown page, where I found this humor "Charlie Brown" book in the ditch, and Snoopy sleeps the night away in a dream among stars.

It was "rats" of a late start and only one café open, Sunday at nine, Morning, do I feel new? Little swelling. I almost could run old Anarchist Mountain Pass. After vigourous grinding, my ability realizes that these few half dozen miles call for relaxation on remaining seventeen stretch. My strides are long and carefully placed. Inhaling through nose every second step, and exhaling through mouth in this repeated manner. I approach cautiously as I view from the left highway cliff, Osoyoos. White board-painted shack resembles haze from the mountain cool and the bright warm fifty-above valley weather. It's beautiful here halfway up the Pass, looking down on my conquered serpent highway.

"Hi, you're Hank?"

"Rightto"

"Could we take your picture?"

"I guess so."

A postered guinea-pig, don't know whether I'm expected to stand, crawl or squat. Tightening the Dutch strap, I heave the pack higher on the back blades to relieve the padded straps cutting the shoulders. The sun sets low as I reach the twenty-mile summit, with a frosty wind of a promised cold night. Most skiers have descended the 4056 elevation pass, after a soaker of a sunny Sunday on the Bridesville meadow slopes. My nylon soles crisp loudly the silence of the highland fields that pads the appearance of a dancing Northern Star. Such an evening! I round a gully curb where on the sloped field side, A clustered Bridesville sleeps.

Teapot seeps, moist steam arises and the dead, dry underbrush volcano tepid to ashes. Now I, with one side heated, finish a raw burger-meat with garlic onion, and topping for dessert, is two sliding raw eggs. From a frosty crisp morning to a raw, windy afternoon, I reach Rock Creek café and consume a large hot dinner, then wage the bill hurryingly, pursuing my days destiny. Sun descends five hands high, while two counterpart crows are casting hideous laugh-calls. I harmonize in tenor as they shriek and fly from the high-top pine. Go!

U laughing many, for this is not a joke. The abrasion plateau winds, starch my windburnt face. I realize that it's too cold for another night of outdoors. Between the midway sawmill and the village, I meet Jeff, teacher and journalist who invites me to a hot home-cooked supper with night lodging. I cross the despoil tracks where now only freight is toiled. Supper hungry smell, I watch Jeff's three kids. "I want ice-cream and pie now. I'll eat supper after." When asked, they all receive dessert and that's the finisher for supper.

"Would you sing a few songs Hank? You're leaving early in the morning?"

"Yes, I'm forcing the summit walk to Grand Forks."

Such evening of friends with songs I love that protect me from my lonely journey.

It's a short sleep till 5 AM and leaving quietly, I lock Jeff's back door after scratching a note of thanks. The northwest, full of "Aurore Borealis" bed flowing-quilt for morning light. Man! It's nippy way below, as I creaky enter a small forest valley, aware of hidden eyes, and whistle the tune of remembered last evening blues. Dawn breaks, and two hours later, I enter Greenwood. The sign reads… found in 1897; hope there's a café.

Twelve miles up with as many down, sits Eholt on the crest with harsh mingle strides, and I'll have these boot-heels for repair tomorrow. I pass the second row of sharp deer prints carved in belly-deep snow; your plight for food I avow. Haunched by a twigged flame on Eholt crest, I'm heating a given yester-evening home-cooked beans in jar, with A half dozen of dry frozen tasteless wieners. The white-coated green forest on this sheltered sunnyside of the mountain, chaperones the black imitating crow. I'm high above the Russian-farmed valley, coiled among the low cascades. Commune settlers have very large and few houses, with eight windows on the west front. How many rooms, I wonder? Both feet dried after the third and last solution foot soaking, I change sweated socks and worn hiking boots. I'm set for five miles to the city of Grand Forks.

The limits beyond he glides
When rain is promised in the clouds.

THESE BOOTS WERE MADE FOR WALKING...

With Hank Gallant in them, that is exactly what they do. The pair in his hand are a tailor made pair, while the ones on his feet are being broken in, "You have got to take care of your feet," says Hank. Bt the time he reaches St. John's, Nfld., he will have worn out several pairs of boots.

Daily News Photo by Dennis Goff

Chapter 2

TRIALS AND TRIBULATIONS

Yesterday was to B restful but with A school visit, and patching clothes, I feel somewhat like my worn hiking boots. Languoring the narrow elevated curbed highway to Christina Lake, and viewing those high beyond stamina trials, old Monashee stands. My mind looks back on yesterday's task of appearing at A grade eight assembly. Mr. Hentoff invited my presence to B questioned, from why to where and when. Young Fred Popoff, the chubby school comedian, explained that in Fork City, if your name doesn't finish with "off" you are not with the "in" crowd.

The Jacksons', a modern bush pilot, his wife and three children are emotionally attached to the spitfire cub plane, and their caring mood to invite me for hot chocolate and sandwiches is great. The old glowing sun is descending; one hand from Christina Range appears sickling for tomorrow's weather. At the lake shop, I stock my food rations, and trying hard to escape from a group of kids following on bikes, I find a high dry bank on the lake shore. Pitching pupper and seeping "McQuack," my observers question every move. After A partly warmed supper, then singing with a throttled voice in the frosty evening air, everyone agrees on an early shut-eye. So long my friends, it's been good to know U.

February twenty-fourth: Before the first light gleam, the small frozen tent is packed by nipped, numbed fingers. Turning mind-power to the walk, forty-seven miles of Blueberry Paulson Pass, I round the farewell curb of Christina Lake. I stand to ponder the beauty-break with the fading moon on the East glowing ridge, and the flaming dawn casting upon the scuttered hue, with vertturquoise brushing the drifting ice. The silhouette slated mountain peaks.... this beauty I hold and watch for many a minute. I climb the winded shrubbery-covered south slope of desolate glitter in this early morning frost. A few cars I meet, with only one long hauler passing, who stops and offers me coffee.

"I met U A week past on the Hope summit. Ain't U discouraged or sick of walking yet?"

"No, it's my adventure."

Eating cold sandwiches prepared yesterday and sipping very small quantities of water, I lose no stop time. Steady stride crossing the Paulson Bridge, the spruce-hung two-hundred-foot canyon holds the wild gushing river from snowfields above.

With four hands of daylight, I have reached the 5036 Bonanza Pass summit. Resting, seated on the pack in five feet of plowed snow, I despise the rotten hard descend of twenty-three miles down to my friend, "Jim's Café." The evening falls with cramped run-away steps when suddenly, four hot-rodders attempt robbery. The yellow livered punks, but I am saved by A trucker who saw the summit's unfairness. He brings his air brake rig to A fast stop and emerges with the long bar wrench, chickening the apes to their Ford get-away. Ted agrees; it's not animals but humans I should watch. The Rossland branch-off sign, numbers sixteen miles to my rest. If I didn't know what A charlie horse was, I do now, both rubbery and hard muscled legs folding in various directions like A sprawled calf on ice. Zero cold will not awaken the exhausted body. I have to keep plugging on miles that are long and slow, but I'm finally helped by A customer to the Kinnaird Café door. Jim hurriedly unbuckles my gear and I'm fed hot soup stimulating the hazed mind. Just look at those blood-torn knees. I fell many of the last sixteen "hell-miles."

"The seraph fauna blow of claws, gray hawk now lifts the bloody squirrel."

Steaming hot water... vital force … my lifeblood body. Hours of rest, cleaned and freely stuffed.

"You're beyond all thanks and kindness."

"Welcome Hank, but I would want one favor; would U drop A card when U have A chance?"

February twenty-sixth; my first splurge… porter steak Sunday dinner, two scoops of mashed with much vegetables and milk. It's A rare tender cut. Seated across in this Purple Lantern booth noting my bored fixity, I'm thinking ….funny, the old girlfriend I met yesterday on the Castlegar road. These new shoes were mailed here to consume the two-hundred miles that it will take to break foot-print fit. Irving Bisswac, U didn't have to say, U knew I always looked like this, even if I loved your sister, in year sixty-six. In the mind cave-dome of dwindled thoughts and tired from inquisitive questions, I daydream-stare on the Columbian River and disappear in the fog.

Leaving the Nelson scene, followed like A piper by A handful of young kids, I cross the Lake Bridge and walk the North Shore road, where the evening North-west wind blows from the Kookanee glacier. An unhealthy haze rises and falls on the unfrozen lake, debating then deciding on the Balfour 3A route, one-hundred miles longer than the South 5820 foot Salmo-Creston Pass. Darkness falls again and I desperately try to reach the last lake boat at ten p.m. crossing. "Could I take another summit punishment on this early stage of my long endurance walk?" By fifteen minutes, I miss the bloody boat; I walk the Balfour streets to inquire at the lighted home.

"Yes, what do U want?"

"Pardon me for interrupting your evening, but is there another ferry crossing tonight?"

"No, I'm afraid not."

"Oh. Would it B possible Madam, for me to unroll my sleeping bag in your garage so that the damp zero weather won't affect my back?"

"No, we don't allow tramps on our premises."

I explained my walk and her husband and son joined in A ridiculed snicker. I turn to the directed "males out-house", feeling snubbed and timid with the realization that I'm in the wrong place at the wrong time.

Morning arrives; it's goodbye, John-house. The road leading to A dung rainy day is shaded at intervals by tall willows and cedars. It's early for the migrating goose, in formation from Sanca Lakeshore, and a dozen and one velvety trumpet calls break the reposing timbered Purcell Mountains. I try answering, arousing only the gander's caveat honk as they gracefully swim to the lake center. "I have felt free, or can I attach something that even the V flying geese cannot be?" The few moments that I have spoken about my journey in the six years of dreaming and planning, gloom and ridicule I've often received. "The young people of the Attic Coffee House,.... did they understand or laugh?" I wear the Attic crest patched on my sleeve. "My mind is not chained."

From peaceful rest to cursed dampening rain, I change strides listening to the fog quiet among abandoned summer lake cottages and the shrieking blue jay.

"Good morning."

"Hi."

"But where have U come from?"

Such beauty, as she emerges from her sister's home........ A melting smile.......soft clear brown eyes....golden ponytails sheltered by A black slicker sou'wester. We talk and walk.

"I'm going to the store A quarter mile ahead."

Her friendly concern, yet unconcern, pick up my morale.

I forget the insulting quotations name or sleeping in A toilet trash can.

"Are U really doing what's written on the pack?"

"It's mild weather for the Kootenays."

I don't like answering pretty girl's questions, even if she doesn't believe me.

Dripping mouse-tinted sky, the evening falls upon this washed twenty-second blue remote day. From the highway, I perch on the highest lakeside boulder, being watched by the kingfisher who flutters his feathers above my head on A rampike spear. Forcibly eating wet soggy sandwiches, I watch old fuzzy dart aggressively to A ripple silhouette where minnows leap to join the falling rain. With a brief dive, his mug beak swallows what he caught, and then with daring anticipation, he glides to another relish watch. I am left alone shadowed from the serene graceful snow-ivory peaks. Leaden dusk falls, ebony run-off streams gush to the silent aged lake. I splatter like raindrops….. down that never ending highway.

From where the shriek, now silent, I stand powerless, wondering with A back chill….. will it spring…. am I the prey? There's the thing…… old bastard yellow cougar, crouched now behind A rock ledge high to the left. My cap is standing skyward on shaggy should

B cut hair. B Hell if I'll camp along here. Speed striding the distance, I feel the weakening chill of being followed. I carefully place each step, not to show my trembling limp that might bring on the lanky three-hundred-yard charger. Gripping tight the two-battery flashlight in my right hand and the small Swedish six-inch blade hacker in the left.... is my only protection. "Are U stalking me, or only curious?" I calmly cross to the right lakeside shoulder, then rounding A small willow-bend, the Sirdar Hotel blurs its light view. I rush the approach at A jog, horrified by the shadowy lurking creature. Crashing the pub door open that hit my triangle guitar pack, I explain to the owner who charges out in the rainy evening with his loaded rifle. But realizing that the cat would not approach A lighted house, he returned.

Breakfast being large, my mind mingles with more of the horrifying scares of yesterday. My thumping heart is now calm, and it is good to B awake. Away from the mashed battle dream, I was hiding to escape in A large pebble field from dive-bombers lurking in the sky. A termination to my toss crawling body, trying desperately to reach A distant foxhole, I wake to find reality in various forms... A sculptured horror dream.

The days have been short; with now approaching spring, my hand measured time has to B change as the sun sets longer in the skies.

March third: A spring felt month in this seasonal climate valley, trying to reach Cranbrook in three days. Now leaving Yahk on this frosty clear morning, after A consumed remedy breakfast of great variety, the mid-day sun thaws to A slippery grease-like form, on the soil road shoulder. Ah, it's good, even if I feel A bit spring feverish.

Crystal mountain stream water, how fresh to drink. I Soak my sweaty feet in potassium permanganate solution from A small plastic soak pan. Watching the above crossing of a logging road bridge, the powerful Vermilion ten-wheeler shakes and thunders the ancient tribal forest valley. "Progress, are U the breed of destruction?"

A log Pioneer Museum sits on the South bank of its man-made pond. Mrs. Barnhart waves me in for tea. Pleasant people they are, Bert and Joyce treat me to a winter tour even if the pioneer structures are seasonal. Old Simon "Baby Child" follows.

"Do U like cats? Think how much company Baby Child would B."

"Oh, sometimes Mam." I'm not telling her I despise Siamese, They're evil-looking and two mouths are one too many for feeding.

Four hands high on this draggy sunny afternoon, I have steamed spicy chicken spaghetti, served by Tom Murphy from A large thermos container. I am seated on pack above the highway splash and melting snow cutting.

"U must B joking; driving from Kimberley to serve me hot supper?"

"Right Hank, we heard you liked this sort of meal, so my wife cooked this dish."

Today is my lucky day. Beyond the feel of spring, there are the blossoms that grow from people's kindness, the love heart-doing on which some flourish.

I walk into dusk dog-tired, with no fuss on location; this vicinity has choice camping hide-a-ways. The frozen snowed-over lake lies A couple of hundred yards from the webbed heavy green underbrush, used as A mattress bedding, pitched and settled. McQuack boils the tea. Wondering, will my kidneys become fragile with the sharp attack from outdoor elements? No curl to the steamy smoke, which rises arrow skyward above my pendant pupper, beyond the tall bushy top spruce. The soup, now heated, has an indescribable energizing elasticity that conveys warmth to my perspired body, relieving the tightening muscles from the miles of fatigue, and the icy sweated underclothes.

In the frosty-white spiked hung twigs, I hold my almost empty extinction matchbox, one to go. I tear up my old map, wrinkled from the road conquered. The engorged flame reveals the twisted sketched, "Moyie", yes, that's the lake out there, twinkling under the moon's rays from A high altitude cold night. Tea hot, two, three cups, with lots of sugar cubes, and two dry hard tacks with A can of bully beef with remaining rations, plus one pure chocolate bar will do for my energy at break.

Smashing the quiet silence with hardened callous feet, the will and body has strengthened my inner mind. Minutes stretch to hours beyond the curving highway view; there's to be A café, I anticipate.

The grizzled drab roadside alder, towering nude in the dry cold light wind, hangs A high courtesy for summer bird nesting. Reminding my growling stomach with the final chocolate sweet, dinner I have to reach soon.

Now seated with A double burger, plus a maple milkshake and an order of toast, I feel rested. Sixteen more miles to the city, I hurry A pounding walk trying to receive the echo-call from the painted Canyon. Various mornings when frost padded the dry, cracked mountain slopes, I've raised my twin voice when whistling A walking tune; this answer was my only true road friend.

Approaching Cranbrook with the bosom sun setting one hand over the Eastward Bull Range, I have an overwhelming greeting. Dozens of cars follow my journey while entering, where the head officer and fourteen Girl Guide Rangers invite me to A prepared ranger banquet supper at the Club House, Water does A million wonders, washing and preparing to face fourteen lovely girls. I'm nervous; what will I say? "Good and hungry". The lodge room is tacted with a laughing tickle. "I look like the road," but it sure brings out girl giggles. Honored to the banquet's long table, the shy guest is seated at the very end, feeling doubly nervous. The "entrée" spread is served.

"We read Mr. Gallant, about your liking Italian foods."

"Yes, A week past on the summit journey, and I mentioned European foods."

Joining the whispered stares, and not showing that spaghetti is only A moment's craving, I feel foreignly stuffed. With the after dishes greased and tomatoed, pushed to a cross pile, I emerge with the git box for A sing-song.

Late evening finds the abundant loveliness vanishing, and the lodge house is darkening. Lonely but warm in location, I spread out my freshly washed clothes and dry out my tent, sleeping bag and pack board.

"Old fifty-pound pack on my back, oh Lord."

"And I sure ain't gonna B walking back."

The Sunday morning haze, as people search for peace and joy, I leave the lovely yesterdwelling. Painted, dressed, put on their best, to some A vast contest. "Good morning." Boy, I raised A smile from that churchgoer!

How wonderful feeling, the soft fluffy pure white wool socks padding my itchy feet. The faded clean clothes and showered body, had me counting Lynda, Beverley, and Kathy; instead of sheep last night.

I turn east on corner T, route 3, wanting to touch the rigid Bull, Steele and Fisher Mountains, bright in the mid-day sun. An artist's skill brush. With a lowered view that separates I from freezing white water, the Kootenay River flows hidden below its pine-laid banks. This gaze flows tears, as being able to touch. Now witnessing such a magic landscape, I ignore many stares and questions from passing autos.

"Fred, Fred, how are U, old buddy?"

"Piece of cake! What A small world Hank. I didn't believe U last year,"

"Did U move from Slocan, Fred?"

"Yes, my Father and Mother are Russians (rushin), but I'm taking things easy."

"Oh U crazy duke, U're the exact person I met on the Duncan Dam."

"Yes Hank, U should not B so lucky. Farewell, and B sure U visit the Slocan Valley when U return."

"I will. Bye Fred."

After A blazing sunset which fires the South-east face of the North Bull Mountain, I pause while branch bedding my tent in A small spruce bush on the outskirts of Wardner. Oh! How I wish for summer with no frost chill or tired thoughts. This afternoon. Mrs. Rivers invited me for the Boss' birthday dinner. Their friends, some friends, and nobody believes my walk, but I'm not proving anything, it's my trial.

March sixth: To wake at daybreak from the collapsed tent, damp and chilled, I'm standing in knee-deep fresh snow, shaking out guitar from the wetness that might warp or unglue old "Gibson."

Packed for a journey I enter the highway café, Oh! Good hot strong coffee, a stimulant for the blizzard outside. To B full, to B rested with deep inhaled freshness. Ahh! It's the first smell of the onward flats, but I'm afraid of blowing snow.

The hours pass as I charge, facing the homeward wind. Eight storms swept miles, visibility zero, and not beyond two-hand reach.

I settle for Jaffray; A late hot beef sandwich. Wrap up, tie down parka, lace up boots. Hot digiddy! Old sappy sol peers through the flaky clouds, and the temperature drops as the day narrows. I now slowly stride the uneven passage and view A large sawmill. The forklift driver stands watching while I pass. He now takes the broom to the quilted fresh fluff, sweeps the lumber pile roughly, then works the back wheel machine to the box car for loading.

I am allowed to use an elk hunting cabin by its owner; A little old kind lady.

"They're closed for the winter Son, but if U can heat one up, you're welcome, I heard of U from Nelson, U look to B honest."

"Thanks mam."

Room number four. There is A strong smell of damp musky clothes and A few mice choppings. I leave the door open while stogging the cast iron stove full of Time Magazines, Weekly Stars and good hunting guides.

Scummy North-east winds wake to shake the cloaked evergreen forest from its old yesterday's snow blanket and add A fresh fall that fires the days challenge. "Would I tremble, shake or die if I ate that snow?" I'm careful not to damage A leg by slipping on this high side of Elk-River bedding. Plows are working in the storm. It's safer walking the green moss-covered brown brook rocks. I join the road once again at the river "Portage", where there's A mountain spring flowing from the small crack opening on the massive slope. Depriving my sweaty feet of the socks and boots, forcefully holding my right naked foot in this congealed crystal stream, is A shock, but do the feet feel great! Marching on through flakes, pounding both feet to warm, I'm fixing my glare on approaching the Rockies.

A fifty-eight Ford, with three nuns, approaches.

"Good-day Sisters."

"Hello, are U the person, who….?"

A frozen-standing interrogation. "Farewell Hank," with a parting comment of: "You're not afraid to starve?" Now why did I call them "Sisters?" I must've been brought up this way.

Fernie, B.C. covered deeply in the sparkling snow; wired news reveals welcome Centennial guests, as the carnival and slope fun begins tomorrow. Welcome, welcome! A badge is pinned on my black cap. I'm escorted to the King Edward Hotel for A free room given by the Centennial Committee.

Snow dry gopher wind
Shoots clouds
through the nest of crows.

LONG DREAM...

Hank's idea to make the cross-Canada trek his Centennial project started in 1963, but the ambition to walk the length of our country came to him as a child.

"As a kid in school, I used to dream about walking all the way across Canada. Now I'm making that dream come true."

It wasn't just a plan without preparation. Hank started studying how he could make the 4,585-mile journey along the Trans-Canada Highway while attending a Vocational school in Prince George, B.C. He climbed mountains with students from the University of British Columbia in Victoria for fun and training. Last September, with his vocational education nearing completion, he began doing road work, 6 hours a day, in readiness for the walk.

my project but now that I've made that, I'm confident that I'll succeed," he said while in Moose Jaw.

"I made 47 miles in one day- and it took 16 hours," he said. "But I did that from necessity, not by chioce. There was nothing but wilderness. That was in the Rockies."

He stopped in Lethbridge for four days to earn money as a folk-singer. "I made sixty-five bucks singing 15-minute spots between shows at a Lethbridge hotel," he said.

MOUNTAINS ROUGH...

Then, in early February, after a final good-bye to his UBC friends Hank left Victoria.

"The mountains were the roughest part of

31

Chapter 3

MOUNTAINS AND MOLEHILLS...

T he morning's radiance is blurred by the hollering storm. Beyond the City center surrounded by neat white-painted houses and paling fences, an aspiring faith house stands. Covered coldly by the much fallen snow, its spire seems to pierce the world-laid blanket. Ascending the concrete steps, leaving the old house packed out, I enter the still quiet, revealing my snow brushing efforts; yet, I'm almost alone. Kneeling for A few words, then hurrying out to the nearby Liquor Store for A bottle of sweet Trinidad wine and filling the goat gut skin, I leave town.

With all brute meanness, the cold dry blizzard is forcing my handkerchief-covered nostrils to gasp A sweaty chill, as I turn often to shelter my breathing from the headwind challenge. A mid-morning soup and ham sandwiches bring elevated tolerance. A few motorists stop, trying hard to convince themselves that I wasn't true to my cause.

"You're joking!" "Come on, get in, we'll take U to the mining town ahead.

"Sorry to disappoint your frolicsome fun, good day."

"You're crazy! Get your head washed."

Natal; A black-coated streak on a white mining town, settled in A small valley floor where notched midnight holes contour the smelly look of A coal town. The soot coated snow furrowed street has many different languages; Italian, French, English and German. Working partners are laughing happily arriving from shift, tromping sooty snow and talking about work jokes and greenhorns.

A large, eight kids French Canadian family invites me to enter for supper. Would U know, there on the table center, A high rise three-decker pink frosted birthday cake! Flaming the ten small candles before the introductions, blessings and wishes. Now we gab the "Français,"

"Marie, my wife, she likes the guitar and songs, and all the family like the music; I enjoy mining songs, for it's black down there underground."

"What A set of lungs, Emily!" "Are you sure you're ten?"

"We have phoned the hotel owner, and he has A free room for U sir."

"Thanks."

"It's inhuman for someone to sleep out in this storm."

"Well I did it before, and probably have to sleep out cold in the future. You're very kind."

"Before U go, would U unwrap your guitar and give us A song?"

"Happy birthday to U, happy birthday to Emily"....

Key number six; complimentary room from the Kokanee Hotel.

It's A bright sun kissed aurora, with sooty icicles forming on the entrance porch of the Canada café. On the only unperched stool, the order is given to A dark haired Italian-speaking Canadian girl, who jabbers with her off-shift customers in A foreign lingo about her love life. "She's fat and slow."

Michel; A twin apparel town, A mile east from Natal. Boxcars are loading under large chutes, also ten wheeler dump trucks. High above the highway, A covered conveyor belt carries the coal to B graded and treated in A large square aluminum sheeted building.

Mid-day sun seems noticeable through the huge fast blowing Westbound clouds. Forcing strides bent low, the sky joins the Crows Nest Pass, and the blizzard is met. "Thank Christ, I have reached the Province boundary and the crest of the Crows Nest Pass." In blinding snow blowing, I tromp A shelter in the six-foot drift. I prepare for the task of sewing the "B.C. coat of arms on my ball cap", here on the Alberta-British Columbia border.

A Chivalrous toast, A triumph boldness; I'll walk this road for much to go. My hazy mind I'll clear with a sweet taste of wine; hearing the laugh of the east wind's tone reflects the three-century "Coureur de Bois" song. Dancing son of the wild; he has traded for beaver and pushed over rapids and chutes. Some had twelve wives in A valley so blue. His horses and dogs were faster than most of the chief's band. Five hundred pounds, twice told, have passed through sore hands. No place where A man enjoys so much variety and freedom as here in Indian virgin land. "Huzza! Huzza! Pour le père sauvage."

Brought to life from the exploring days by the reality of honks and stares of passing motorists, I rise with strength from the past. Mush, mush, the hard snow bed and the blinding efforts attack me. A bogged Hound Bus, spins, hoisted on the shoulder cutting. Later in the evening, the winds have died to A sparkling cold. A gaping motorist passing has ditched his Chevy. Standing in white fluff leveled ditch, waving and cursing my strange appearance.

"Go on with U, if it's my fault."

March tenth; A cold moderating fifth day of continual snowing. Funny some people; I do what, and try hard not to bother, but being questioned and mocked-at, seems beyond tolerance.

Blairmore town café, I blindly enter for hot chocolate. How long will the wind funnel up through the Crows Pass, placing large scars on a bony frame that fights with determination against nature's elements?

The east town limits standing to the left, A winged carved black pair, "Welcome to Crows", and the snow blurs out the remainder of the sign, "Nest Pass." Can't even see the last of Pinnacle Rockies. Should buy shades to help this walk amble snow blinding effort. I walk east, holding ready to ditch-jump any snow bound sliding traffic.

At a Chinese café in Belvue, I have A greasy cheap pork-chop dinner. Shouldn't B choosey when sufficient calories are so vital in this windswept cold? In meager shops, I wheel and deal for food rations.

The ground drift is small with the evening clear, painting a double vision of the rising full moon. A picture profile trim on the scrubbery spruce-coloured hills, adorns the brush effect of the silhouette's hue. "Goodbye Mountains, so long". On descending A long slow grade, I'm met by A young chap with his hands full of groceries.

"Too much snow on the lane, have to leave the car out here. Would U care for coffee sir? Mom will have A pot on."

"Sure thanks, I need warning up."

"It's not the greatest weather, Lethbridge gives ten under Fahrenheit."

"I felt it when the sun went behind the peaks."

Coffee talk, horse breeding, yarns and A few sandwiches-heavier, I leave. On the way out, I'm shown the prize stock; all saddle splendor, then black stud stands. Twilight swords the beaming moon; now four hands above the sage hill, where below on sickle formed Lumbridge Falls, the dancing diamond angel calls.

The lobby is empty in this small hotel, but the bar noise shakes the door. I unstrap, stand the pack before entering the pub, then look for the proprietor to get A room. "What A Smokey rough looking hole!" Approaching the bar, I'm stared at from all drunken angles.

"Pardon me, are U the owner? I'm looking for A single room for one night."

"Yes, there's one, wait."

Approaching, is A handful of mumbled singing, rough necks.

"Seen U in the papers kid, you're A crazy bum."

I grin and ignore the insult.

"He didn't hear me." This gets him mad.

The bartender places the key on the counter.

"Four dollars."

Before I can reach for my wallet, one of the louder rednecks slaps fifteen bucks, saying, "That's my room."

"No, I asked for the room!"

"I'm telling U to move! We don't cater to crazy phony bums here in Alberta."

The bartender growls for them to sit down, and picks up the fifteen dollars.

"Sorry, no room. I had forgotten he asked yesterday."

"Yes, I suppose."

Then leaving madder than fighting, it would B suicidal to fuss in there. I'm surviving mental suffering; how can anyone B so ignorant and animal like yet raise their children up to love humanity? "Can this B possible"?

I blank the thought when looking for A small spruce bush. I cross A field to tramp down, bed up, lay down and freeze round.

Peering my head from inside this no-good sleeping bag that's wrapped tightly with two ground sheets and coated with a six-inch drift of silty snow, "it's torture no matter what I think." Get out, scrape out, shake out and cook out. Paper and Twiggs feed fire heat. How cozy I want it, big and burning, for I have survived this outside night and it's twenty below Fahrenheit.

I notch the fifteen odd miles, plodding another screaming Northeast gale sounding miles on million acres, and frozen dry gray clad. I can't see the so-long Rockies; they were A friend and shelter. Hand hitting warmth with smothering bandanna breathing. I stand the wind on high.

What A green mean dream! It's landed. I alone under this bush; what do they want? Hope I'm not found. Crunch, crunch, they are standing tall over my pup tent, huge green men.

"Please...... don't take me; I have to finish."

"Please! Come with us Hank, come." A big reason to B frozen this morning. Sure, hope I don't dream anything like that tonight.

Afternoon sock change and A sipped cup of tea, sway the ample walk to Pincher Creek. Entering A main street hotel, inquiring about A night singing stands for grub money, I ask Murray who advises, "This isn't an entertaining pub."

"But would U wait? I'll call the boss."

Returning, he smiled and said……

"U got A free room and can sing tonight if U can drown out the noisy drunks. If you're good, you'll pick up some bread."

"Thanks."

The early Saturday evening crowd is more observant than the eleven and twelve hour tussle. Twangy blue and dusty songs with A droll cry of sweet old mouth harp, I gather the biggest sing-around bunch on Mountain Road.

Twelve whole dollars to carry me on.

Ain't got A care, or A dime

Blue skies above, this land that I love

That's why I'm roaming on, singing A song, whistling A long.

Streaming aurora beams the first morning light; such A breathless stillness twenty below. My departing warning from two R.C.M.P. Constables is to watch out for the Reservation Indian. "You're crossing the Piegan grass today, also watch the West dark clouds for the northern". Thirty-three pounding frost bitten miles to Fort

MacLeod. One has to hurry beyond three miles per hour to keep the body considerably warm. The brightness reflects the lazy low rolling hills, my first revealing view of the past stormy week.

Brocker Reserve town; elevators peer high above the snow white flowered sage hilltop. Miles before reaching the Reserve I'm warned again, which turns me off. With the steam rolling from the doors and windows, I see how cold looking are the handful of shacks. Further, down in the ravine section, two husky team fellows join me.

"We live at Fathers, back up that gorge. Your Hank; Newfoundland bound?"

"We're having A small game this afternoon."

"We play hockey with the Pincher High. Charlie, he's right, I'm center."

"Have U A rink out here?"

"No, A pond, back of brother's ranch. Want a play?"

"No, I gotta hit Macleod today."

The only car besides the R.C.M.P. patrol to stop and chat is the chief of the Piegan Reserve, his wife and his daughter.

"We watched U coming, lugging such A large thing. Should have A wagon. My wife got this hot plate of dinner ready and a container of coffee."

"How kind!"

"Well, it's A long walk from Pincher to the Fort without A hot meal. We're not that viciously savage, eh?"

I'm cheered on, photoed up and left alone. No manipulation of names; these kind people of yesterday who are classed and corralled in the bareness of districts. The Piegan, a name which means "poorly dressed in skins", were allies with the "Blood and Blackfoot". A strong and free tribe, they rode like clouds in the fresh wind for centuries. Riding their Pinto-Hammerheads and hunting for the food that used to B, is now left with the brand name scalpers that was introduced by the White Europeans. These proud people, now at white carnival stampedes are flowered and feathered far richer than their forefather's custom, who are gaped and mocked at, for only they know their heritage and culture.

The wind-burnt penetrates deep, entering the bone with A toothache effect. Contouring A lazy snaky running brook, if follows among the willows and thorn bushes. I mix water and wine to help with thirst and stomach cramps. There on the distant flat stretch, beaming with the farewell sunset, Macleod brims twenty-seven degrees under, Sunday chill.

My hotel room is the cheapest. Stumbling tired to the opened café for A hot beef supper, I am crowded by the Town Mayor who is the owner of this plush eat-room. My swaggering pride is crushed by piercing statements and the feeling of imposing in entering this town and café.

"U have A considerable amount of publicity, and now that you're here, it would B good for me and the town. Your room, dinner and breakfast will B taken care of for my publicity."

"Thank U, I don't need your type of hospitality, good night."

Refusing the free hotel room admittance, the rejection carves my tense stomach. I lay in bed sick, sick of towns, sick of all but my walk. If there was A shelter out there, I would've camped, but I'm in another hotel.

The rubbed easy-low bumpy hills are deluding the plains search ahead. It's beyond very cold, with a bandanna tied over my nostrils and mouth, helping not to freeze my lungs. I force the half sixteen miles to Bridge City, and A four-burger dinner lowers the funds to seven dollars.

Dusk has fallen with the temperature dipping all of twenty. I'm on the west bank gorge, sipping coffee with A steelworker who gives me the low down on Lethbridge. Descending with the obscure gut feeling of dropping from sight on A moveable surface, I slip curl the winding bends like A runaway bear wanting to roll down. I reach the flats below two miles from the city. The sixty-six miles of brisk weather in two days has seasoned my physical endurance. The dark relating structure of A burnt smell brewery on entering the city, I arrive at the first Lethbridge Hotel inquiring for the owner, "Luckier than crow, I'm given A four-night stand, singing during band stops in the hotel bar room. I have A free room and meals with ten bucks per evening."

March fourteenth; trying to relax my tensioned muscles in A hot bath, I realize that a boring four days is in store. No day work could I find, even with the publicity interviews; I have to make fast money to carry me on. Dropping the hiking footwear for heel and sole work, I'm patching and repairing my gear.

Now the evening drags in with my fixed appearance between the Western Band sets. Most hazed eyes follow the skinny, shaggy dressed traveler that slowly mingles through the beer crowd toward the center stage. Some point, nudging their friends and the whisper is clear.

"Is that… can't B him we saw on the news coming through the stormy Nest Pass!"

"A mere child, no taller than our son, makes me worry about him away in the army."

"He's so skinny, he'll kill himself."

"Ahhh, when I was young, I did walk twice as much as that."

"Good evening folks; my name is Hank Gallant; I'm A long-distance pack walker strolling this Country from West to East. I've stopped here to work for A few days to boost my food money; I do hope U will enjoy my self-made-music."

The evening excitement is washed away quickly by A morning phone call and the twangy uproar from large city hotel advisers. I catch the burning scapegoat of Liquor Bar publicity, and I'm honest to this hotel, as I'm threatened for mentioning the pub hotel where I'm entertaining and being interviewed. This is against Alberta Liquor Laws. "Bull, get lost."

"The Green Beer Blues,

With St. Patricks' shoes."

The final night plucks the twangs and the Irish rosie songs belt the crowded pub to A clapping singsong. Packing in retirement, minutes after the final pub appearance, I'm sixty dollars richer counting my tips. Can't wait to burn those itchy feet.

The mixie works
One green back pay,
Mark the plains
A long, long day.

HE WALKED...

article by Don Myers, Moose Jaw

It's a long way to Tipperary but it's likely that Hank Gallant would walk there if it were possible.

With the Atlantic Ocean separating Tipperary from the 24-year-old native of Prince Edward Island, Hank is trying to do the best possible.

He styles himself as the Centennial Walker and intends to stroll to St. John's, Newfoundland, touching all ten Canadian provinces. He left Beacon Hill Park in downtown Victoria, B.C. Feb. 6 and took two months of walking and working to reach Moose Jaw.

Now, he's back on the east'ward trek, earning money to pay his food and lodging as he goes.

"People say that there's nothing to see on the Prairies. I've travelled from coast to coast four times but, in those four trips by either bus, car, or train, I never saw as much altogether as I have so far on this trip," he said.

45

Chapter 4

CHINOOK PHOBIA....

The moderating windy weather in four days has risen fifty-five degrees, and it's A clear light chinook of thirty-five above. Splashing the slush laid shoulder, listening to the seeping snow, it crumbles and decays like A wet cardboard from the warm southeast wind. My reminded thoughts of leaving A friendly town, seated on the East gorge slope with smiles and waves, I vanish with valor in the sphere of haze, watching for wind signs. Most fields are strip farmed, preserving the top soil from blowing away in this slow rising flat, without any shelter from nature-wide.

The six-hands sun long shadow, clears the warm smiley welcome to Coaldale. The boney tall snake charmer converses to the following children. A free café dinner with A beautiful centennial plate, is my most astonishing gift. Glancing over my shoulder to the high grain storage elevators, I wheel to grab one of the following kids who without noticing, walks out on the highway from the gravel edge in the path of the oncoming car. Smoke, rubbery smell, and screeching steel drag with many swear words, the driver is cursing his head off; must B because he didn't run over the child.

"Now U chaps, better high-tail-it back to town and stay back from the road."

"Bye-bye, good luck!"

"Why in the hell are U walking the road?" roars the motorist.

"Goodbye."

"You're about the fiftieth car who either stop, honk or wave."

"Hank, you're invited to have dinner at A Tabor Café. It's on the town."

"Your friend Mr. Anderson, has his home open for U. Hope my joining in the last of the thirty miles won't disturb your walk into town."

"Piece of cake" is great to have A policeman along. It's protection after dark."

"My patrol partner bet with me that I wouldn't walk these two miles."

March nineteenth: A late start from Johns' on this quiet lazy Sunday morning. "Church-going families are dressed round, puffed up, or coming from." The calm frosty night has wrapped A tickle damp quill chin-hair on every outdoor structure. I receive delays from motorists, with questions and camera bugs; the lovely pose from three Lethbridge Nurses, smile "Cheesy", and the cold morning has vanished to A song.

I stumble from an old gutted shack across the C.P. tracks where I sheltered for the night. The frozen figure enters the Grassy Lake Café, and gulps A disturbed breakfast from staring eyes. I'm to give A quick visit to the school kids before hitting the highway. "Oh Lulu!" What questions!

"Aren't U scared you'll get lost?"

"Do U have A compass?"

I heard the cry like A coyote afar.

"I don't know baby, I don't know."

Following, spitting, bucking my house pack high on the shoulder blades, I'm covering A good three miles per hour without over forcing. The mirage plains reveal the long gray dismal barren flats, and the ghostly grunt silence of the million buffalo phantoms, tramps and paws the frozen stubble where they graze with their hinds to the Northeast wind.

A dry ungreased squeak comes to A halt; A forty-nine G.M. half ton, red with brown-splattered-cow-manure-fenders. The driver, humped back, tall-skinny, peers over his wire frames under A greasy peak cap, with a squeaky voice.

"Hop in, son; I'm not going far, only A mile or so. It'll help."

"Thanks Mister, but I'm walking across Canada; I won't accept any rides."

"Across Can...a...der?"

"That's right sir, the writing on my pack tells you."

A long pause, while he stares at A lone burnt spruce in the opposite field. A chill runs up my back…. "What will he say?" Slowly without motion, his gaze pivots to my structure. His eye level peers over his glasses at my high laced hiking boots, and like A revolving light-house-rays, it pierced my body and mind. With jest, "I have work to do". He jerks chugs A jumped three-gear shift takes off. I roar and roll with laughter, being perceived as A fanatic by A gradually fixed spectacle glare.

The clear damp piercing March winds blow from the Arctic, sweeping and screeching through the power lines like my guitar tuning, It's A long mild grade from Bow Island to this highest farmland in Southern Alberta. As I view the long descending sections, miles to the North, I change to the lighter footwear, seated on A spilled pile of grain. I'm surrounded by small sparrows, snowbirds, and a crow perched on A nearby fence post. Posted against the horizon miles beyond my reach. Medicine Hat's industrial smoke joins the clouds. Old Sol peeks through the evening ridge one hand high, not helping to warm these cooled soaking feet in an overflowing roadside stream.

"You have eight miles to reach the city, Hank." "Come to the big hotel; I'm the assistant manager; you'll have A nightstand there."

"Thanks, I'll play for my accommodation."

"Be seeing U in A few hours."

I walked thirty-eight vanquished miles, and my hazed tired sinking body was rejected from this phony hotel appearance. The assistant manager didn't notify the hotel.

March twenty-second: The hard windy, #3 route now joins into the Trans-Canada Highway, doubling traffic. Occasionally, the swallowing wind tunnel blow, from large oil tankers and cargo transfers causes unsteadiness. If caught off balance by A large fast-blowing diesel smoke wind, I'll end up into the ditch, swearing at the large vehicles and my triangle pack.

My friend Joe; how lovely, got your letter at the Hat. Prince George is yet the same drag. "What about the mocking Alderman? Do they yet call me A Moses?" Let them drown in their watery words; I'll cross the Strait on A ferry.

I can watch where I lay each step, or view the sage tint auburn ranchland that often has been turned by the iron plow. The cypress hills, A southern distant evergreen view which tapers to A rolling mold, pleasures me while walking among these windy hills. A cloudy sunset passes while I watch for an abandoned building to sleep in. There will B no hot tea this evening, for I don't want to burn this granary down. I sit in A wheat bin, playing my guitar softly in A cold damp night after forcing my way through A side door with the hunting knife, prying A wooden crossbar. Later the moon arises, haunting the corners from its peeking view through the high small peak window. "I wonder; will the rats allow sleep?" I'm very comfortable, wrapped in a sack and tent, covered with wheat.

The chinook blows A forty warm snow eating wind. I was lucky that the sleet came in lightly and iced the surface, A safety against blizzards.

Dear Mom and Dad. "I hope they get this letter for Easter." It's my first notice to them about the walk.

A boy presented an Alberta Crest from his hockey sweater. I leave Irving, heading east towards Saskatchewan; I feel empty and alone, and blue meant nothing till this day. The outer shell conversation and meeting people, frustrates me. I only converse within, hoping not to talk out loud to self, but with the help of my let-out guitar hanging from my shoulders, I slowly dust in the south wind, singing the "Highway Blues".

Last night was spent in a fresh warm outdoor brush; my first comfortable night out since the forest valleys. The sun hides behind rolling-dark northern rising clouds, four hands after dawn. While sitting down by the Alberta Border monument for shelter, I sow the "Coat of Arms" next to British Columbia. It is only minutes later that the winds of Chinook hopped to the icy northeast.

Many days have flashed since my departure; I never count miles ahead or even ponder on the thought. There's an elderly couple standing alongside their blue fifty-five Chev. I cross the highway to the café, where the owner snarls at my order.

"What are U trying to prove anyway? Most people go to Good Friday Services, but U just walk. For what?"

I gulp both burgers and milk, pay A buck and beat it the hell out of there. I hear the grumble acquaintance; "What's the youth coming to?" "Now what brought on that?" Maybe the little old couple; I better move. The early holiday travelers buzz the highway noise exceedingly, and I try not to notice gapes and stares from ski-strapped cars to three-ton farm trucks. I view the fields for dashing jackrabbits. Along the highway ditch I've counted four since leaving Maple Creek; they stride, hopping from A burrowed hole in the snow where they feed on the covered grass.

Further east towards Peapot and beyond, I watch the south stretched Cypress Hills move in colour from white to A chestnut brown. The hills are alive with herds of antelope. A protective park for these tiny bouncy creatures.

Having stored my food rations in the pack pouch, I leave carrying some wieners, milk and bread for supper. Finding A slough east of Tompkins, I hunt for A green foliage bed pitching. After the water is steeped for tea and washing, A rumbling noise trembles the ground. I crouch listening as if the vanished world has come to life; darkness rolls the beauty-beast of A living kingdom with sixty million buffalos that roamed these plains in the seventeenth hundred. Small relics of the fauna gore with white bones mostly memories. There, vibrates the smoke stack highway tanker. I now wash my dirty socks and purify my burning feet, then crawl to A back chilling sleep.

Easter Sunday, March twenty-sixth; it's A gray hazy distant sun-rise with no feeling of holiday spirit. With pack strapped, and vitamins swallowed, I point for Speedy Creek. Setting one's mind at ease, and whistling A sharp tingling tune to today's gray noticeable landscape has less scenery for my lonely view. "I would like to B home, but this is such A beautiful experience!" If there was a company, A friend. No, this would not B good with my circumstances, either he or I would Be A burden.

Late afternoon visitors from R.C.M.P. highway patrol, to Mr. Sommers A Saskatchewan flying farmer, later swoop low among the power lines on two fly passes. Many disordered laughs, with mockery remembrance and leaving hurriedly after A café meal. My blood boils when I am mocked. Now seated-resting while sharpening hunting knife, so I may cut this hair, I wonder…. Do I look better or worse, or am I trying to please them?

Monday after Sunday traffic, the bored ski holidayers return with gapes and questions. Wish I could walk these fields; there's too much snow and barbed wire fences. The antelopes from Antelope Town reprieve and spring-leap over low-lying farm fences. How gracefully without strive they meet the far rolling horizons.

"Rick Duchene."

"Pleased to meet U."

"Here Hank, is A little something U may enjoy."

"Breakfast, great great!"

"That's fresh farm-cured bacon, lots of eating; taste one of these slices."

"Sunnyside eggs, yum!"

"Webb sits A mile below this grade, south. I met U this morning and figured you'd like breakfast."

It's late Easter Monday evening and I top the thirty-five-mile jaunt, entering Swift Current with the big excitement. I'm invited to A large local dance with Betty Kimble men.

It's a complimentary royal room on my day of boot repair and rest. I crawl out of A soft warm cloud-floating bed with bent tension swayed; the north moist wintery wind sweeps the down street gorge across the railroad tracks. Speedy Creek lies dry and frozen, much like friend Wayne had described the Current. I visit Mrs. Brown, and now I'm being delayed on my way to appear on the local "Sports News" by A young R.C.M.P. Constable. He searches my pockets, counts the thirty-five dollars, mocks and threatens to shove me in the "jug." I'm in A hurry to reach the program, "but he doesn't believe me." "But I'm late Sir!"

The dirty sticky-blow, swallows the outskirts town café. Nature has once again erupted its fluff inners. Would I call white falling snow dirty? But there is this parasol tilt mixture, and drifting snow has tainted human refuse. Within viewing distance of the following highway fence, I buckle down and walk partly side-step, so the strong wind won't catch head force into my large triangle pack. At A café garage, three hours down the highway east, I get the low down drag from another owner while eating two donuts with coffee.

The afternoon howl coats the burning freeze structure with A blue shield that bites with needle-pick-pain to loosen me from my hardened courage. Turning from the highway heading north, one mile down A small entrance road to Rush Lake, both feet are frostbitten and the front of my legs are stinging. It's A light bite.

The Sweeney's are more than hospitable. Seated in A bedroom with both feet soaking in cold water so that the frost pain will ease out, the leg leaders are tied in A hundred knots. Both feet turn bright indigo, and there's swelling under the dried callous leathery skin. I later fetch A pail of warm water from the café kitchen, for the hotel has no running water for baths. Using old fashion earthen-ware bowls and large tall crockery pitchers is sufficient for A warm sponge bath. I'm soaping sweaty salt and relaxing my body and mind.

After A night of frustrating entertainment from A craved wild rock-west-ern-young audience, they reach their fill of A high strung electric guitarist, with fiery piercing eyes and vibrant thunderous beat notes. I happily emerge from the yodeling café to my cool frontier stage hotel room, happy with the results. "My feet are OK".

A tasty wildlife breakfast is similar to yesterday's hot partridge supper. It's delightful. A cold antelope roast steak sliced thin, cheese in long sliced blocks, with rye bread home cooked, and golden churned butter from A Jersey cow, topped with a jar of wild strawberry jam.

I leave the hotel in great admiration of their kind hospitality. Commencing the gray-still of the morning walk to the Trans-Canada Highway by-pass, one-half mile down the flat gorge, I notice dark gray falling clouds from the Northeast, as the turbulent blizzard swallows Rush Lake, which I left only an hour past. I realize it's too late to heed the warning against a stubborn determination of daily continuing. I should have waited the day, but now I can't turn back to retrace the steps. Trying the bandanna on the nose bridge, and my parka strapped tightly, the body structure braces for the big snow blow. Hours linger beyond days, while I struggle from smothering and being tossed in a road dike with the pack. I gaze through snow packed eyelids and steamed glasses, gnarled in A bent over sway. Twice, the canvas wrap-sheet that covers the pack and my guitar blows loose, flapping like an untrimmed jib. Pain freezing my hands, I tie the pack and remove snow from inside the Gibson.

Eight hours later, the ghostlike shape reaches the high grain elevators of Herbert Town and Shelter. Reaching A café porch door, numbly the right hand extends its naked bleach. My double-felt and woolen mitts blew away, lost, never noticed from the cold. I'm treated kindly with hot liquids; tone and strength returns after A rest and a hot beef dinner. Listening to conversations within this town. I realize it's A German Canadian settlement.

I find A three-dollar hotel room, then later in the evening the caretaker from the Paterson Grain Elevator brings my mitts.

"I found these blowing about the door step."

"Thanks."

"Danke schion."

The night of turmoil erupts, and finally in the early morning hours with loads of snow bound passengers hugging their hot coffee cups, I realize that it's A plain hazard. I settle to wait for the storm out with Hans and Heinrich.

April First: Much has been said with wasted time. I force on in the cold morning air, dodging traffic in-around snow plowed drifts and stalled cars. Realizing it's A storm trick on April Fools, my wallet shows twenty-five dollars for food money. I sure need A solid diet. Morse then Enfold Saskatchewan-shine gleaming in the after white quilt. The tall elevators show three towns ahead, with the distance of nine or more miles between each.

The thermometer holds at zero, and Chaplin stands A memory of A sweet girl who walked A mile entering the town. Her jealous boyfriend runs us into the ditch with his beat up half ton.

That red ball glow, sets on the snow pad plains, - calling, dancing, and motioning to the wind that rises when he sets to shine on the West.

After the eight P.M. supper is digested, I leave the café to sneak to an old abandoned house on the east entrance of Mortlach. There's one room that has good windows, so I wrap up to bed down on the dry floor.

The fifty-seventh day from departure finds me edging east on the Regina plains. I should make the city late tomorrow, now that the endless flat is reached. Stepping down the frozen gravel shoulder, I whistle sharp notes in answering the many large flocks of "joli blane" snowbirds, and small clusters of English sparrows feeding on the refuse tossed along the highway. A young boy of ten approaches, struggling the three-foot drifts in the field to meet me with a beckoning motion.

"Would U care for tea sir? Mom and Granny and Sis want U to come."

We crawl up the gateway, then on reaching the Ostler home, I'm greeted with warm hearty handshakes, - tea with sandwiches, and treats for the highway journey.

Finally, I leave the newly worked on four-lane highway to talk with A C.P. track repair crew, passing on their spotter.

"Got A place to stay tonight?"

"No."

"Well, we're on route checking tracks to Moose Jaw, should return soon."

"Follow the underpass tracks into Belle Plainer, then wait at the track camp for the crew."

Leon and Nicholas, and names like Herman and Tom, A Metis from Prince Albert, are working, sweating and singing under these narrow cold moveable box houses, A drinking coffee crew, cheap whiskey, and playing high poker hands, passes the time of a long desolate night. The punctured kerosene lantern flames the entire room, before it's finally tossed out on the snow. We evacuated for A half hour; it is beyond midnight when I crawl into the chill sack.

Belle Plainer, its quiet type country houses, some shingled, others mortared or brick, show various European culture designs. From villa to town with communes of Mennonites and Indian Reservations, Ukrainians and Germans', these are the people who spade this land.

After six hours of sleep, the crew grumbles out of the cold bunks spitting and yawning, kicking the coal skuttle.

"Sure is A heavy breakfast, Hank."

"Yes, good for A horse."

Departing at seven for the twenty-eight mile hike, I hear the howling freight whistle, - welcoming the towns, that destiny calls for freight transportation to the lake ships. Chinook phobia vanishes as I walk on. The greatest threat is the northeast, where most blizzards erupt. The wheat city I view, must B halfway through the plains.

Pushing, side stepping A path through the busy downtown Regina, I collect my five postal letters. Finally, I reach the pursued Y.M.C.A. The large white face electric clock points to six and A half past, while I patiently await the arrival of the desk clerk and the assistant manager.

"What can I do for U?"

"Sir, my name is Hank Gallant."

Then the explanation continues, and ends with A bored glare from the manager's fixed eyes.

"We don't give charity."

"But sir, I'm not asking for charity, only one marking on A room. I'll work, get paid, and then settle the Y. You're my only hope that I can struggle on towards victory."

"Sorry, it's three dollars per night in advance."

The bewildered figure is slated on cold hard Y.M.C.A. steps. My pack perched against the railing, I thumb through my log, paging for an address. Mr. Jackson, yes. Oh! Harry Jackson on Oster Street. There's no youth hostel and the Y has refused, but good old Harry finds me A basement bed in one of his rented next-door houses.

Lucky with my urgent plea, at ten A.M. I am working at A "Tire Wholesale." A storage and selling warehouse for $1.30 per hour. Casual labour; unloading large tractor truck tires from boxcars to the basement rooms, then loading for selling.

The evenings are spent watching the Chicago-Montreal Hockey playoff games, or retreating to A coffee house. "The Place," where I sing or listen to the words of new creators. Radical Riel, the neck-breaking noose holds your bulging eyes for over eighty-two years.

"Nay! Now U naughty fool," says English Protestant Canadians; "we'll hang U, then name U Prophet who?"

More like fall, the dust dry chokes; no smell of spring. I stomp-kick the sidewalk leaves, crying among the prisoner's plea. It's not the plea of death, but the boredom of waiting for the destination road. Jackson held A portrait of Riel when I met him at "The Place", and held A long four point discussion till two a.m. April fourteenth.

After A termination dragged-day and working with Sebastian, I happily hold the eighty-two dollar cheque. "Chanter, chanter, je finirai."

Bleak sleet hair,
The flat yawn stretch.
Jackrabbit of Easter Hop.

Chapter 5

LA VERENDRYES COUNTRY

Although most muscles are rested in a pretense fashion, this work A-stop brings tension to nerves. I've layed for hours last night, happy; so glad to leave today. The April Saturday fog-frost lifts in still silence and hovers with the fighting mixture of smoke, only feet above these nude intaglio elms. My mind step-boots hit tune with the hundreds of new recruits that pound the early morning square in this gray-dust, smog-abiding Regina. The newly boot heels echo from brick building to stone structure in search of the protesting Riel who hung high for the right of his people. "Who is the hero? Who is the fool?" Consulting matters of vital interest, he helped us create A better world tomorrow. My haunting dreams calls awake; I picture the brown-eyed stare. It's an Indian child, tiny but swollen-bellied, five years deprived of solid food. He has yet no hate but the love of youth. Infant eyes that plead for life questioning; he cannot taste the free meal of his fathers, the buffalo. For survival, could the Indian hunt the white man's buffalo, the steer that grazes the fields, and fill the pole barn? He would B charged to hang for one beast, like "Mighty Voice," who with two of his friends, were given the discretion of burial. They decided to earn A warrior's death and were challenged by the entire mounted police force to die. Oh rats, those eyes, will U let me lapse into oblivion?

From the smog and the noise of the city center, I finally emerge to the outskirts residential section, where an old bearded and cloaked Reverend Teofil Mac fumbles excitedly with his picture bug-click. He jabbers in A high friendly voice that I don't understand; A strong handshake, he points to the Church Romanian and then to his frock. Hank nods "au revoir". The Reverend waves in reply.

I wonder about the elements being so quiet during my boring work and stop. Now it's dark and cloudy when I hit the road, but I'm not crying; I'll take tomorrow when it gets here. Most small spring run-ponds in the country fields are flocked with migrating North-bound birds. Various long beaks, short beaks, fat geese and no wild roast black quack. I'm so hungry and fed up with burgers and stink of bully-beef sandwiches! I finally, in early evening, arrive at Balgonie, hurry to the café, and order fish and chips for supper while watching the hockey playoffs. Quietness falls when I store my chafed carcass in A spotted abandoned barn, where I soak my swollen feet, thanking God for the food I eat.

April seventeenth; in the early hanging frost of A million snowbird wings, my mind is dazed from prolonging the sickness I have caught by sleeping on cold ground, with A poor bed roll. The kidneys are infected; this runs into both hips. Oh well, I'll try for inside sleeping. An R.C.M.P patrol car follows slowly on the right highway shoulder.

"Hello, walker."

"Good morning Sir."

"It's hard to believe U have walked this far." "My wife and I passed U on the Hope Princeton Highway in February; U were dragging along with a cane." "You haven't taken a ride?"

"No, why should I want to defeat my own purpose?"

"Well, all the best to U, son."

"Thanks, au revoir."

The patrol wagon returns to Indian Head Village like A sturdy black tank on watch; one notices the traffic slowing considerably when the patrol is on the loose.

During the afternoon, I leave the thirty or more miles per hour highway blow for a small willow grove on A brook bank. I break dry twigs and set some salvaged cardboard to blaze, and McQuack steeps the herbed Indian tea. Tis good to B sheltered from the wind seated watching the silent flow; it is there, here and beyond, sublimity in senses – the warm glint of the world aglow. The strained motif note of the blues harp answers the stream's melody, and both feet are dry after bathing in tempered water and then held by the fire's warmth. Aaah! Such A good tea to warm the body and mind. The dry crust whole-wheat bread is dipped in steeping brew and raw ground beef with salt and lots of onions. I feel new happiness; the freeness of the Prairie winds have entered my blood once again. I match the wind with laughs.

Old Sol's colorful brush is on the far eastern gray clouds before he sets the red to pink, and the glow is beyond Wolseley farm-sections where the low-lying swamp awaits the dancing frost night bite. I enter the highway coffee spot and order up soup, A hot sandwich and tea, then Wallace Tehler, A school student invites me to spend the night at his home.

"We follow the by-road till we reach the town and cross the C.P.R. tracks to the south."

Wallace, with his two sisters and younger brother manage the house while their father is working in Regina.

"Mom passed away two years ago, and our oldest brother got caught in the draft, working south in U.S.A. He was shipped to Vietnam; we all pray for his return."

Wolseley sleeps like a bear in winter even in spring; it's slow in waking. The Chinese Café holds the young aggressive bored people each night, looking for action, a turn of the tide or trend. The next-door neighbour who snoops in curiosity asks; "Are U going to the French Fair?" I reply: "On way to the Exposition and beyond."

I tune the git box for a song we all know; music is wonderful, tender with sensibility. Feeling close to one's heart, brings friendship and opens the tension outlet.

When I enter the morning kitchen, Linda's breakfast is ready and little brother washed, dressed, ready for school after A hot cake, bacon and egg meal. We all depart in separate ways. "Merci, bonne chance."

After yesterday's fifteen-mile walk, I hold up in Grenfell for A good night's rest with this tearing chest cold; it's A forty per hour windy day. With A stew dinner digested, I sit side-sprawled on the café booth bench, playing the unstrapped guitar. A few of the farmers in A crop conversation are ignorant of the Quebec situation, but with A strong European accent, points the wrongs in Canada.

"The two only large cities I have visited are Regina to the West, and Winnipeg to the East explains, the chap."

"Are U visiting Expo this summer Sir?"

"No, I have no use for the French Fair, replies the farmer."

"Oh."

The Wednesday April nineteenth sticky wet snow holds A two coat colour on the following highway field posts. Both hands are warm under these double woolen and felt mittens. I scan the adjoining fields for A possible shelter; there it is A bale stack. Crossing over the page-wire fence and A four hundred yard dash to the straw, I prepare an igloo shelter in the stack center.

I wake in the morning covered with six inches of snow; it is not the thrilling thought of what the day holds, but the fighting moment of storing and packing my gear with frozen numb fingers. I hurry and drag my apparel rig to the south sheltered side of the stack, now striking A match to A broken bale of straw that is five feet from the snow-covered mound. It's an unbearable cold that cries with pain from inside my lungs. I'm so cold; I don't care if the whole bloody thing burns down, U snow straw stack. Better move fast before the farmer finds me with A fire.

T'was this early blustery morning when I entered Whitewood Café for A burger breakfast and A quick shave in the washroom. The week's growth itches like hell with the straw dust and chaff.

I enter the dismal howl to prod the unseen thoughts that I cannot think, only lift each leg and thrust forward the heavy balanced hiking boot. Up and forward, continually continuing against whatever stands, with today an exception, my courage lacks!

The echo sneak trade of La Verendrye and his sons had opened the portage way to the North West, the Winnipeg Basin and beyond. Those "Coureur de bois" feelers, that softened the hard freeway of the Red Natives, stunned their heritage from those early days on. Two hundred years and more, some arrows cut the air for food; furs were caught and traded for white man's whiskey. The history pages are not all fully blooded like those of our southern neighbour whose philosophy was, "T'is only good Indian is A dead Indian." I follow the snow-bound shoulder, paranoid by the question that an old Indian once asked: "Why, when we the native retaliated it is called A massacre, then when the whites butcher, it's an attack?"

In the scream of my mind, the blizzard shades the bulky structure that enters the sheltering whirlwind of A tall grain bin. Partly numb beyond exhaustion, my hunting knife enters the parting between the double ramp doors, and edging the barred two-by-four from the notch, I push the door open. Inside A grain bin with the sleeping bag wrapped with tent and wheat, I warm the night await, watching A handful of sparrows flutter in the high peaked window.

The calendar shows April twenty-first, high above the Wapello Hotel kitchen door, as ancient as this structure looks. There is A friendly smile from its owner and A shapely Prairie girl who prides herself in her artistic walk, while serving my breakfast. Her smiling welcome would like to keep me from the prolonged stormy weather, but in leaving, I'm followed to the door where she stands watching with a smiling farewell. Vanishing from sight in the morning blizzard and like A Greek column, her profile waves A love worth engraving.

I march on, stride replacing steps, entering A world of hardness where nature's fit survive. Those wild ducks that stand on one leg curled and fluffed in their feathers, waiting for the pond to thaw and grass to grow. This most B puzzling, on their migrating route, to encounter winter and severity.

Red Jacket Café has hot soup for A two-bit price on A bowl. Most stops I make during A miserable day are for warmth. It's three-thirty on the cobble shop clock when I enter Moosomin Town.

"Yes sir, what's the trouble with the footwear?"

"I would like A heel job and new clickers."

"A lot of walking on them?"

"Some; I find the gravel shoulder hard on the heels."

"Why don't U walk the blacktop?"

"Can't. It would burn my feet out in A week; there's no give to the asphalt."

"The boots will B ready at five p.m."

Inquiring at the R.C.M.P. office, I was given A basement bunk in the old abandoned jail.

Shorty the cobbler has caused A happy dream in my night of sleep in rat bin basement. He worked one hour on my boots and wouldn't charge; such A kind helpful spirit. The morning songbird sound of this April rise has A glowing shine. Sol sets one hand from mid-day half when I reach the Manitoba border. It's the third coat of arms that is sewed next to the Maple Leaf Crest. Raising my rusty desert can high for the toast of triumph-trial on the bleak plain. I head on into Kirkella, then Elkhorn. I arrive at dusk, looking in telescope fashion for an inside lodging. The Town policeman allows me to sleep in A gathering room in the back of the fire hall. Basing my money shortage to three dollars per day, I have extra for one night's bath inside A cheap hotel before reaching Winnipeg. A choking feeling I'm locked in; someone barred the door from outside. It wasn't the policemen. Rotten luck, how do I get out of here? After kicking and hammering for two or more hours on the heavy door, trying to wake the Sunday sleeping neighbours, I'm set free at ten, which destroys the thirty miles planned for today's walk.

The rays-warmth has filled the air, and the call of spring return once more with the seeping germ-coated snow dripping from earth of zenith drift roll.

I smell the sour perspiration that cleans my body pores. How I wish the stream water was suitable for bathing, yet it would B an oily wash. These brooks have A slick, and the bank willows are coated with the black muck that's carried from the oil derricks by the runoff.

Bob and Penny wave A welcome call from across the field, A quarter mile from Virden. I slush the ankle-deep mud of the thawing stubble field to enter A circle of friendly people. They sing the night away, and I depart after breakfast from that soft Chesterfield, with A six-signature battered-dollar to carry inside my guitar for the remainder of the walk.

The mid-day sun has me carrying the heavy parka. I arrive at Oak Lake School with the invitation from the principal. Now to enter A school, why did I say yes? I'll never know. Those introspective well-oiled minds, prying at the wildest odds to shoot for the clouds. I hold calm but not cool, with both knees shaking. It's not my thing to get stared through; most believe me, some are bored. I'm not spitting or breaking my neck explaining reflections of the affair. Happily accepting the generous offer to A free dinner at the Highway Café, that boost the energetic strides, I meet the whiz-blowing transports as hours speed toward sun fall.

Beyond the slit-light gleam the fog strip dream disturbs my rest, waking in turmoil and sweat with the sleeping bag A furnace trap finale. Frightening weather on the endless sea of plains, the lack of friendship and squalor dream after yesterday's thirty-three miles, I crawl in an abandoned C.P.R. tool shed. I'm heading for Brandon, debating whether I will shed these long-johns and insulation lining with this strong April fooly weather.

The Carberry Hills have low lying gravel canyons with small flat plateau of spruce groves. Crawling over A high snow gravel cutting to the entrance of an abandoned pit of   A sheltered tall "grove", the warm spring sun joins the licking flames of my tea-break fire. Oh! Its such weather, A bit cool, now that the itchy Stanfields lie trampled by the roadside mud, east of Brandon.

In early twilight hue, the perfect camp location notched, I climb up the brook bank with McQuak filled. I enter an underlying webbed spruce thicket, break an armful of dry branches, and light the fire for the tea to perk. Tramping the wet snow, I break some low lying green branches for a mattress, one foot thick, seven by four feet wide. The tent pegged and ropes secured, I roll the bag inside, wrap both ground sheets, and place the guitar as A headrest while sipping tea, and eating A bully beef, cheese, onion and mustard sandwich. I hear the traffic whiz and roll drone, less than four hundred yards to the south on that parallax black snake endless highway.

April twenty-seventh; emerging through the forenoon fog clouds over rolling green spruce hills, I level off after midday burger lunch. There to the south and sunset lies the cast mould of the Carberry Hill forest. Once again entering the wheat section of the Plains and meeting the crying winds of the gray afternoon, I bend forth with determination drive; "never will I quit"! Their faces laughing red; "How many miles? Two weeks in the winter cold, you'll quit!"

"No, no, no! I'll walk all to the finish, or die trying." Much alone, knowing that the many U called friends understand not, they roll with the laughing stock. "Friends are few and far between, alone my pallid floating dream."

In the midnight sun evening, my tired mind whirls on a pivot stool while the dish pans clang in the Austin Café. I stare the red hot beef dinner with double spuds and an extra vegetable blob, looking me in the face.

"Pardon, what time is the hockey game?"

"I believe nine p.m."

"Would U know of any location where I could watch the finals?"

"Well, most any home in the town sir."

"Dollar sixty-five, there thank U ma'am."

To try one more house takes more than courage, for the last two doors slammed shut in my face when I asked, "Would it B possible,

Sir, for me to watch the playoff game in your house?" "No, U can't." Boowam! I guess it's silly to want to watch A sport I like so passionately.

Old foggy blue pain and emptiness reaches my inside tears. I leave Austin door-slaming, spurned in the darkness that hides the midnight cowboy race. I find a partly empty grain shed in the high corner of A field, pry open the shut door and hit the wheat for a night's sleep. I dream about the master puck handler, the graceful tall bone structure superstar. Good night to my only highway friends, the gophers, who I call to wait when they scurry to their burrows in the ditch and shoulder. "Could we talk?" "I can carry you, little gopher."

There's A heavy pressure; I spring out from inside, smothering into A complete dark horror, as tons of dust-choking-wheat pours through A chute. I keep silent as the running dry ocean rolls to my waist in depth bulk. Now the farmer roars the tandem away and returns to bolt the shoot. Searching in scared mistrust to B found in an unfriendly section, I dig hurriedly trying to locate my lost covered gear pack.

Five hands sun, April twenty-eighth, sitting accompanied at Bloom Junction Café by an R.C.M.P. Constable, the chills glide my backbone as relating the thought and fear of the morning experience. In the gray dim afternoon strides, my eyes level to the high many coloured grain elevators of Portage La Prairie. It looks welcoming, but I hate to walk through the city. Could this B the centuries past, with Fort La Reine on the Assiniboine River bank awaiting me?

The rich duck, loaded with trading furs on the cargo canoe, leads A pack of Indian tribe-warriors to wheel and deal with Francois La Verendryes and son. Aaah! It's A happy day-dream on the road side walk; it is not A fort but Prairie Portage, and the causal mix-up of the journalist and interviews that leads to A free highway hotel room.

I'm determined to watch the three-thirty afternoon Montreal and Toronto fifth playoff game. By A wild chance crossing the highway from A late breakfast, I meet A friend.

"Pete, how was your eastern love?"

"Just silky soft; all my love baiting, promised A cherished week. Rats Hank, U're dusting the road!"

"Thanks Pete."

"I've gotta go, trying to reach Calgary tomorrow noon."

'You won't come and watch the game?" "I'm leaving after that."

"Well Hank, I'd like to, but I have to report for my job tomorrow afternoon." "Cheerio, good luck Hank."

"The best to U Lagire."

The sun has no measured view in the gray low clouds of early evening, after the Leafs whipped my favorite team. The mocking laughs of the jet-set green suited clan echo like the noise of the river. Through the night, I plan to walk. Ten miles passed in the chilled east wind. A man emerges from A yellow house, and invites me for tea.

Between dusk and dawn, the northern lights dance. I lift the fence, and feel a cold chill of someone close by, breathing over my shoulder ear. I once did hear that night was made to sleep and play. Now I'm hunting in Benard among large square block brick buildings for A shelter from the east. It's early morning with both legs weak and buckling. I realize that it's either A hospital or maybe an orphanage. Inside A small storage building among dismantled swings and seesaws, I roll out sleeping bag on A bedding of mats.

In the tint dun light of A cool Sunday, I wake from A warm summery clover sweet dream, to cry with biting pain at the numb picked fingers that tie all what I carry on moulded pack. I reach Elie Hotel with its door locked and A quiet whirl of dust on ghostly main street. I pound on the door.

"What do U want?" "Sundays we're closed.

"I'm sorry, but I need A room bad."

Relating experience route, the proprietor treats to hot coffee and cold beef sandwiches, then we both retire to our beds.

Fumbling in the darkness of A cold unheated room for my frozen blue jeans, I leave Elie at early five a.m. All weather station warns of A Monday blizzard as I dust out and into the wind for early capture of Winnipeg. The first four hours before breakfast pass with energetic ease, and nature vomits its sticky white girdling scene. Food I swallow in gulps, bent, rushing through zero visibility. The remaining twenty miles with smothering pain of each minute arrives, and the snow hangs to freeze on my blue jean legs; I vision the warmth of my relinquished Brandon long john underwear. Traffic crawls to A stalled blurp. I blindly fall head-long into the ditch, slipping and crawling to the shoulder. Later, I realize that I would B safer and getting less wind down in the ditch following the fence. Between large blows through my snow steamed lenses, I see huddled wild geese tucked in A feathered ball. One could reach over the fence and touch these beauty fluffs.

Mid-afternoon, I enter A tunnel-like coated street with cars bogged, spinning burning tires, and buses picking passengers from street center. Inside the city, I walk the miles in frozen posture; I'm sheltered but yet exposed to the laughing stares of the five P.M. home walking workers.

Beyond the trees
That mighty breeze.
North flying geese.

20 MILES PER DAY

His daily average of about 20 miles per day hit a low during his walk between Swift Current, Sask. and Moose Jaw, 110 miles apart, when an April snowstorm kept him to 10 miles in a six-hour walk The following day, while the storm raged on, Hank stayed away from the road.

As far as singing interests, Mr. Gallant said, "I liked Bob Dylan before he added rock to his songs." He also voiced support for Canada's Gordon Lightfoot.

"I've written about 20 songs and hope to get some published eventually. I sent one in on the Centennial song contest but arrived too late. Still, the Committee said that the song was quite good."

Chapter 6

THE VERDANT MOULDED LAKES IN THE WOODS

S uch outer warmth from mellow south, with none the happier, while waving farewell. I peel and unsnap the inner lining of this heavy army parka; good U have been for keeping warm in the coldness of winter. Hanging liner on post, and heading onto Highway Number One, the land of green spruce bend-road is thrilling with adventure. Beyond the city smoke-stack profile flange, where the gophers peek, I wee wee in the free comforting wind; I dodge A few flying cars with pretty miss, boy I'm shy. The centennial blue flag, tied lower than the Red Leaf "Drapeau" is on A small bamboo fishing pole, laced to my pack frame. I hope this elite profile causes less stopping from conning motorists, who try their unbelieving outmost to bribe me into ride-taking.

To the steps that are fast, with double lanes turning to one, St Anne lies two miles to the right, as I enter the tall spring poplar land. I hold high the goatskin bag, squirting long red streams of water and port, without swallowing Adam's effort. I spear the tent in A cut-out grove on a dry dead poplar branch pile. The drawing flames paint A scene of A hundred gypsy camp fires, as I steep the green tea that warms and cleanses me. The guitar I play and sing in the echoing gray wild, before the sprouting grass. Stars glare bright and diving rain-swallows cry A chill-ripple in my cooling blood, as I lie on army mattress aired soft beneath the sometime smelly sleeping bag. Much beauty in the misty clouds of the fleeing night.

The moment's freeness from my warm sleeping bag to the damp white frost fog. I pull on the stovepipe iced-touched blue jeans. I jog around in bare woods, picking dry twigs that flames A burnt smoke red on the half dozen turned-up wieners.

Three hands sun; shoulder strap padding is cutting neck leaders with only this extra weight of the flat air mat. The forest evergreen I've reached, and suddenly I cannot see the Plains. Happy are those steps among sliding low hills and frog-croaking ponds, as I drink sweet rock-pure water. Questioning: Why do I have to make lots of cash at this adventure? Most people scheme money; doing this walk for A challenge is crazy, they say.

Oh, how the May winds blow, with mating shriek birdcalls, measuring their perching grounds. Inside an Esso Café, forty-five miles from Winnipeg, Acres joins me with A hot beef sandwich.

"You's got your fishing line?"

"No."

"Well, U better pick one up; coming further east along them lakes, there's pike, cats and brown lake trout." "You could feast on A fresh catch."

"Yes, I should."

"Hey Pete, U got A small line gear back there in the store? Put that and both meals on my tab."

"I appreciate that Acres, but I can pay for my own takings."

"As A gift son, I don't mean to B pushy, but if I were younger, how quickly would I join U, for very few others may feel the happiness of A summer breeze adventure.

Prawda after Whitemouth River, and sitting in an elm crotch, dangling over A large whirl pool on sheltered side of bridge, I try pork rind, but A hopeless cause in the red run-off. The beauty smells, when miles of garbage stretch onward as motorist dump and disobey all litterbug signs. In early afternoon sun warmth, as my vigorous stance show in durance, I'm posing duck-like, one leg up; I wish people would stop click taking. I feel suddenly like screaming.

Closing in on midnight Tuesday, I crawl over A page wire fence while the quarter moon whites and opening through the large bushy gum spruce. Yards from the highway rumble, the nights resting blackbird flutters and fly's blindly in the silent void. After brushing teeth and holding my fried calloused leathery feet in A cool basin of water. I rest the exhausted minutes before slumber. On the dancing peaks of the flowing heavens, the Northern Light fiddlers play. The smell of spruce with running sap – the youth does grow like hay.

What A damn fright, to wake with nosey sniffling, deep inhaling herd of Holstein milking cows nudging my tent. I awaken from A fiery dream on falling cliff; I yell out, shoo off U hairy goons. If cats are curious, what are cows? Swallowing the vitamin pill, I walk on to East Braintree store against A wall of northeast wind. The shaking tamarack tree squeaks, and the few birds that fly are low. I bite into A tasty hot-cheese sandwich roasted, held on A crotch green branch an hour before mid-day. I sing sweetly and the ground I walk is trampled from the maddening highway. The sun hides in A west haze, cooling to join the damp wind. Rested, stuffed and eager, I leave Falcon Motor Café, forcing the five-mile distant border. Wiry tangled spruce trees are sprouting like toadstools from the weathered cracks on these small boulder islands, and kingfisher is perched above the indigo lake. Each bend and across the highway has A plush azure vista. I'd love to hop on that high boulder island, camp on the flat crest under these small spruce and throw my line for A breakfast trout.

"Hello, I finally found you. I'm Roosevelt Scott, two-wheel biking the road."

This chap without dust on his grey bike jacket and jeans is peeking soberly from under his low hauled sunshade cap. Extending A strong handshake from A one foot balanced position on his ten speed, we chew the fat, and plan our obscure camp position hidden yards to the north side lake grove. Walking the two miles returning to the Falcon Hotel for food and A few yarns, we sit in the yellow-lighted adjoined lounge looking bleakly at the insulting stares thrown at both of us.

Sipping A milky brew with A sweet-fat tasty cheeseburger. Roose remove his cap showing his neat trimmed crew cut, and I display A chiseled gouged block hair-cut.

"If those things bother U, put your cap on."

Roosevelt followed suit.

"You have every detail planned and saved for this route?"

"Well, I live in Magnolia, Alberta; I made big money on construction in the Peace River." "I'm taking three months including Expo."

"Hey, U bums, why don't U take your caps off?"

"Don't answer Hank, he'll fade away."

"Too bloody lazy to work, living on us."

Then he grabs Roosevelts cap.

"Would U please give me my cap?"

All hell breaks loose among beer glasses crashing, when this over-fed, loud Manitoba Branch Hydro Superintendent, tears Roose long peak sun cap in two. Four slaps and crunching smashes, then flattened, with Roosevelt standing over him.

Very lucky in escaping. We sneak, walking yards from the highway as loads of reinforced goons hunt to beat us into pulp. In the returning bush tangle flee; Roose lost A part from his camera, and I A mouth organ holder. The small dry under spruce branches flame up in our hopeful cover from the highway carnage hunt, as I steep the green tea, and pleasantly rest, ready for warm sleep.

The soft, moist breeze blows through the cracked rock shield from the Dakota and Nebraska cornfields. Roosevelt catches the early budworm before our friends, the red robins, hop chirps, and gulps it down. Huff puffing the catching flames, we seep the McQuack tea.

"How about trading cereal for pemmican?"

"Yum!" "Where did U get it?"

"White man's good at skinning buffalo."

Leaving the sappy-smelling safety of the forest tall, Roose ponders the memory about last night's swinging cap scuffle. He carefully fold-packs each bit of tiny equipment. Farewells are like the moss that would sprout where the young learning fawns will feed. My hand waves "bonne chance", and I watch the shiny new bike disappear among spruce winding bends to the east.

To the victory of Manitoba Arms crest I sew on the sweated cap, I'm surrounded by the immense forest, disturbed only by the "wild willie" speed-pushing motorist.

May seventeenth, after A mid-afternoon sponge bath standing naked frozen on A log by the soothing lake, I cut through two-inch ice where I relieve my sweated originality; I freshly force onward. Over and around many gray granite hills, some, red rusted with the iron rock veins, I branch-spear two sucker fish for evening supper; they taste more like mud than ambrosia!

Now Thursday afternoon, four hands sun in the lake wood area as clouds fly tree top low, there's promised snow from the Northern cap. The highway housing increases and I reach A burger stop at Keewatin truck rest. My beauty sing throng, marching over the sky hanging bridge, places Kenora on the rock and green slope by the bay lake. There fly the U.S. "Glory Rag," courtesy of the blue painted motel, awaiting its customers in A foreign land. The wet snow sticks on the dirty black frame glasses as I slush-walk and arrive to the hotel's warmth. I take A cheap room to peer-high over main street, before bathing and laundry wash. Many huddled Indians are familiar to the spit stares, as grinding boot-heel kicked in face, being bodily heaved from White Mans pub. Cursed U drunken Indians on his own land that once was love. Below on the snow falling streets where the Kinsmens Banquet holds many that laugh, I cross two blocks influenced by the venom that strain the kinship, where white and red are at their heads. I leave the laughing squaw-men-jokes inside the laundromat washing clothes, as I return to visit the LaPoint family who I met earlier.

"Got your guitar?"

"Yep, where U two heading?"

"A Fire Ranger Station, fifty miles north on A lake." "We bush fly out, trying to live off the land for A 'week or more; should B gone tomorrow." "We'll spend the summer in the wild."

What an evening of song and reflecting music on mortar-coloured walls of A three guitar playing room. I soap A hot water tub when returning to my main street gray room to sleep on staring thoughts, "good-night".

In an unpleasant damp of cold passing days, it's rise with the sun to sleep in the twilight glow when days and miles elapse. I try walk, meditating without feeling of consideration, nor worry blues that may disturb my weary mind. I take each hill east of Kenora, among the crystal lakes into the granite shield. The dead smell of early spring vapour, is rising from the damp cold ground in the sheltered forest where sol peers its browning heat, I whistle the answering bid throng, challenging his nesting area. I wish to B freeze. Are "they" free in the paths of the skyward? Hope the arm of the law does not evict me from this small abandoned unlocked shack by the lakeside. I worry much as I leave, entertaining the increasing kidney infection. At the natural gas pumping station, I'm showed its turbine air compressor and have coffee with the watchman who passed me on way to work the last three days.

At Vermilion Bay in the early afternoon, I try the bare feet and shorts, but resort only to shorts after A few yards on the cutting gravel shoulder. The afternoon steps are placed with heat of rising blisters, and the sun hides behind rolling bigheaded clouds to the left of the Eagle River Bend. I have chosen an old highway road, high and dry to the North of the rumbling highway. I cast A line into the muddy moving river for A breakfast try, A startling gasp, A bloody black bear on the river bend, about two hundred yards away, looking straight at me and shaking his black head. Watching soberly from my highly perched bedding, sipping tea, the bear waddles north-bush way, chased by the enormous mosquitoes that force me to hide behind my screened tent flap.

The maddening rush begins; from the soggy sack-sleep with the warm south wind rain washing my face, I wake to millions of bomber flies, the blood thirsty vampires. Drenched, the rain seeps down my backbone canal, seeking to chafe these carrying legs. Finally, I arrive at evening abrasive end, and A key for A Dryden single hotel room. Challenged by the walk-suffering pain, my self-soul pleads, "Hold on the tub," crying the beauty of rest as the warm water enters the pores to cleanse the turbulent day. I may dissolve in the toe stretching cramps of A mild rest.

The prolonged distance of each village effects food shortage. I skip-hop around the granite boulders, causing much hunger if one has laziness in bean cooking. This food managing has my pack two pounds extra for sufficient-purpose, so I dump my air mat. I try many fishing streams, and last evening fat Wabigoon Harbour I caught four small pike. What A breakfast! Roasted on open spit with dripping vegetable-fat, rubbed on fish steak in the earliest of swamp haze, the bomber flies causes A chanting murmur. The days are like the golden glowed cobwebs that hang on forest in early morning sun dew rays. Borups Corners to Ignace is A pandemonium hell hunger struggle. I forgot my food rations in the tree where I slept last night, but young Danny saved the day with an orange and A sandwich. The "bunk-rainy morning" in the Hanley's family Lake cottage, I drink three raw eggs, six wieners with toast, and A tin-full of steeped green tea from my flat bottom juice can.

In the mid-day, lake crystal water silent-echoes blue with green, as I try my very outset to imagine beyond the painted reverie glint. Could I have A friend? A glass-slippered wearing toad, to ooze my blood for sleep. At A distance in A timber cut, I spot A standing shack. Hurdling the high-piled branches and last winter cut stumps, I reach the one-door, and two-smashed window shed. Settling for A wire spring bed and A five-gallon can to use as A stove, pickled pork hocks, beans and all the tea, I'm afloat in the sleeping sweet flowery smoked-up shack.

May twenty-ninth: At two hands before sunset, I sit among the wild swamp flowers under the Atlantic water-shed sign. All rivers south, flow to the Atlantic, and others follow the evening star-way, flowing peacefully to the Arctic. I pause at "shooting canoe," gush Rainy River Falls, and Savanna Portage I pass at early noon. I feel lost-empty on endless flow, telling right foot to carry on after left. Careful at dusk not to disturb A ready-to-charge cow moose with her calf, and ears twitching, she feels her way across the highway. Most car people are gawking as I help mother and calf with talk and slaps to rejoin the wilds. Wish I could follow that God-heavenly moose, but then, the "no-see-em" and black flies with mosquitoes eating my bones would feast to have me away from the wind tunnel turmoil of the highway.

With progress miles. I'm very happy, singing with the twang droll of the highway dust song inside my cozy water proof tent, as raindrops are falling and wetting life in the sprouting spring.

Potatoes and steak, bread with honey, milk and fruit in the late afternoon. I'm East of Sunshine Hotel in the heat of A burning day when I'm accustomed to frost.

"Ta-ta, I'll meet U at the Northern Falls."

"O.K. Hans, could U cook up the fries?"

He speeds on two miles; this tall American World Cyclist is in shorts and runners, his brown bottom spearing the torment in A balance over his handlebars. When finally arriving at Kekebeka Falls, the sun yet strong in the Western horizon, colours the rainbow vapour of Northern Niagara spill. Hans arranged on A park table, the gold brown tender steaks; the red fat blood dripping fills my tooth of ecstasy.

"Hans U are A naturalist, A cook of taste."

"Believe U me, I was A slop pusher in the U.S. Army, tough, tough."

Watch touching on sol descent sublimity gaze, the red ball sets behind the slow rising fawn trampled forest slopes. There are no spoken words to describe the blue-turned, white-foamed water, declining and tumbling hundreds of feet among the waiting embracing rocks. Hans is in his sleeping bag under the park table, and I'm following the canyon wall in the spruce, away from the park campers. The ground softly trembles with the eternal nature's prayer, and God is thanked with the falling beads of water over Kakabeka Falls. "How beautiful!" I play my guitar among the silent thud-watered trees, praying for peace to the face that holds the answer of life, and all with all.

Early rise, sunshine dawn

Birds are singing, wild dash the fawn

Sounds of thundering, Northern Kakabeka Falls.

There is A tear of happiness in the beginning of A perfect day. Hans, across the park bridge in the white frost morning, seeps the tea singing, "Guten morgan es ist kalt," in A German American drawl. Bread and honey breakfast, and A strong "bonne chance" handshake, Hans speeds his 150 miles A day progress. I'm not sad as I whistle the echo of the forest, for today, mail could B at Thunder Bay. Mrs. Perrin invites me for breakfast from her highway home. She waddles, sweeps me enter, in the northern hospitality way. A whirlwind happy chatter over fresh egg-bacon breakfast.

"Of course, I've read about you, followed the papers step by step."

At mid-day sunshine, I come upon F. Moen and friend companion, dog Bruno. We meet by coincidence of A light year century on outskirts of Thunder Bay. Horray, somebody yelled, it's the Geographical Canter of Canada. I'm happy meeting another highway friend. Moen, A rugged bearded B.C. logger in his early forties, is on walking route form Halifax to Vancouver.

"I'll have U beat by A thousand."

Moen laughs.

"I'm happy for it's our first battle of the walkers." "Why carry such a load Hank?"

"That's the challenge, all of the country with A fifty pound pack."

It's an interrupted conversation. Moen promises we will meet in the West and Bruno his faithful buddy, caries his own food pack, dusting off towards the sunset west.

Entering on delayed Lake Head approach, I look very silly in my cut-off jeans. The steam whistles shriek, and smoke vapour rises from the lake port. Wish I could see Lake Superior of bubble blue. Four, five-year-old kids, smile happy, waving A welcome sign. Dad standing proud in his summer shirt stripes ask. "Would U Hank, sign the family guest book?" The warm Twin City turmoil diminishes the sweet smell of the forest wild into the large brick stone block sphere. The Lake Head is very friendly, and I have five letters to read before the Beard Growing Contest tonight. Sack-out in A free hotel room, I slowly read the news from my few faithful friends. Churp churp, oh, what an upside-down jolly world.

He walked
They met,
We spoke,
More than A hundred years.

Hank Gallant front view...

IT IS A LONG LONG ROAD

Chapter 7

BUSH AND BLACK FLIES

From the observing morning view window in the gifted comfort with loneliness, I look over the smoke-screen haze of A hot June day. The city smog is mingling like A rainbow-coloration among floating cargoes on Thunder Bay. So restful after A Luke-warm bath! Aah, what A "joli jour!" Good-morning, as I struggle down the hotel stairs among the beauty of loveliness, showing off my new beard-growing badge on trophy cap. The Twin City men grew beards, and there were many laughs. Sure was A let-out singing for the crowd. Before sack out, I ate A Chinese over-gorge; that was yesterday, A happy flourished first of June.

There is A struggle piercing through one city, how about A twin? I meet the smiling stares of the pretty working girls, painted too much for the sunshine on the city below. Port Arthur at mid-day hands I have conquered, and as I view over the Superior of water, I turn east to kiss good-bye A wave to the warmest to Cities I've crossed. It's steep and hot, draining the sweat to my white wool socks. The sullen quietness of the mirror Glass Lake, walks me upside down among the tree-top spruce. Roberta sits across the table explaining facts that the View Grand Motel flies the U.S. flag, but that is A mile from here.

"Would U carry my pack?"

"No."

She gave me her address, "England." That's it, she can't cook. I blow A blues harp note entering the parasol twilight, clicking A gravel tune on my new shod boots. Rats! It's great to B alive out here, near A small hill stream under a very large white spruce, warming "McQuack" tea kettle before sack time.

Saturday talk, pray rain; the forest burns dry. Leaping savage-swell fire glowing in the strong South wind from A small friction spark, the diesel freight wheels trigger the happening. I work for hours; hand over shovel, trying like all to save the forest in its youth, which is my home. Ted invites me for breakfast of fried lake trout, and a 35-pound derby-laker is in the cooler, ready for tomorrow's judging.

The crows among many winged maiden angels laugh on acrobatic stand, perched on the Wolf River snag. I've got my line cast out and both feet dangling knee deep, cooling the burnt on poplar shade bank. In this flaming sun, the early morning and late evening is best for walking comfort. After miles and hours are drawn by sheer exhaustion, black West fast rising thunderclouds sprinkle soft fertile life to the "vert" leaf of the living spring. Dorion; may it water your dried forest meadow grass. I walk through the night's warm shower, frog thrusting my tongue to catch the sweet large falling drops. The million bloody flies, who are after my body, have finally washed quietly in the forest stumps. Calloused soaked-feet are held-sizzling in the salt solution pan in front of the high-rise forest slope camp. I'm bedding in the dark late hours, wondering where, when and what was that crashing noise out there. I sleep in fretful dreams, with the protection of a six-inch blade knife under the pillow.

Disappearing around and up steep north shore hills, I gaze at various intervals on the rock-eroded bay-shore of the Superior. The cool West thundershower wind tempers the charcoal gravel, and I change shoes to boots daily, four or more times.

One mile past Nipigon River Bridge on June the sixth, above the highway and muskeg swamp. I rush the tent pitching to seconds with eruptions arising on exposed arms and neck. Inside my tent, the fly battle begins; five thousand bodies mashed by A black trophy cap, and more entering through small holes. I cover; zip up in my sleeping bag, growling at the flying noise.

It's two days after, and provisions drop to A chocolate in the ease of no worry, as I follow the late evening Boreas on my left shoulder. Today I eat A spaghetti afternoon supper at Schreiber Café, then push the miles over thirty, through Terrace Bay. I'm followed like "the piper" by a handful of cycling kids. Probably waiting to stone me when I bed down near town.

One of the happiest days of my walk is to begin in the peeking sun, with a guitar playing, dangling from my neck, putting my heart at ease. The pack, more stationary with the triangle form strengthened, I follow the bay with beautiful crystal granite and pure water trout streams.

"I'm A lonely lonesome traveler,

Looking for A place to lay my head."

I run A few licks, A twang note and A drawling blues harp. There it is, A breakfast pond, before the flies and traffic disturb these angels. Cutting the small top of four eggs to B drank after A large fist size "sun-kist" orange, and tin foil burger fry, the breakfast is concluded. The teacup trembles from the slow-hauling Canadian Pacific, crossing the lake bridge.

The hours are planned with miles that languor, as lake fog sets limitation to the coast visibility. These Islands and rock peaks down South below are defunct twisted creatures from an extinct kingdom of serpents- (now relics in granite crags). I have analyzed my lonely frustration upon the channels of meeting curious people that burns the points of friendship. Loneliness is not being alone, but having constant-people-contact, and friends miles away. The highway cuts the shield, and I follow in the breezy fog. My mind is in tangled daydreams among beaver dams. The moose, stiff-legged and crossing highway is snort-shaking his proud held pointed branch defenders; he's an ugly brown pouch stud. Most of the day, continuing into the night, I feel fresh from the many footbaths and face washes along the highway spectrum.

The town of Marathon is seated on the lakeshore one mile from this road A "walker's wave" after an early morning breakfast. The flies follow like clouds, smothering my nose and eyes: sand flies, black flies, and blood-stick flies. I wonder: Is the northern route

Kapuskasing, all flowery-iced frozen fresh. No, that's too long and I have passed the branch-off. Thirty continual hours and sixty pack-walking miles. I stagger across the ditch, following A wood-cut path to the silent side of A rock bluff; I sleep for hours with little comfort from the blood-bombing insects.

White River, Ontario, has its sign showing thermometer-indication of the coldest City in Canada. The tarpaper stove pipe shacks, shelters the many Indian families around the White Stream town; I can see the flies darting on the kids in the crowded corner structure. I'll do like the rest, close my eyes, and walk on.

Somewhere in the lost count-forest of the night owl silence, I wake not knowing what destruction lies near. It bumped my head. I turn and A black hairy paw swoops inside the tent. "Hey, yah, beat it U bastard, scram." Small flashlight in left hand, and six-inch hacker in forward charge, I unzip and crawl slowly through the flap. The black silence of the forest is shattered with A "woof" and A crashing roll-thud, than escaping to the swale forest below. Wheeling, I turn spotting A glaring beetle-eyed bear standing ... he woofs at me loudly, and crashes off following his mate into the swamp. I'm beating it out of this God-forsaken spot right now, for they will come like dogs after my food.

Obatango and Kebenung Lakes with countless of others, are incarved among the stone shield North of the Great Lakes. It's late evening fog, and rain June of fourteenth, when I reach the glowing motto of the "goose town" Wawa. At the nickle plated ostrich-like goose monument, scary and large in the midnight mist, I pitch tent in A bush behind the Tourist Bureau singing the "Wagoose Blues."

Dear old mother goose in the morning sun, have U any young? But I'll settle for breakfast, four eggs. While packing my soaked tent for the entry into Wawa, I watch feathered starlings stretch the dew worms from the manicured statues lawn. Such swank "quoi" from the goose town. I struck up A fifty cents bath at the Lake View; got my socks washed and detergent. The way out of town is very disruptive. I'm given A lecture on misfits from a Wagoose chap who stirred the town with gossip. He denies his remark that Moen had taken A ride.

"Look, U fellows are all the same, walking, canoeing-bunch in the lakes, horseback riders, easy riders and shit disturbers. This Country is one hundred years old, what dam good are U bastards doing?"

"Look, Mister Algoma, if my Gibson was worth less than A board, I'd drive U… Thanks kindly for nothing."

Shakey from the loud experience and proceeding with debility, I realize, when an advising motorist tells me it's sixty miles to the nearest food stop, that I have been misinformed by the shopkeeper. Finishing the last of the two days ration when I surmount the Agawa Bay ridge, I descend with A trot on the polished-diamond adorned Superior of water. Jubilee indigo with the white speck-flying gull, is food searching the Bay Shore forest. What a camp location! A dream-green thought of my Maritime destiny.

Finally, after an enervating sun-scoped day, it's twenty-four hours since the last breadcrumb taste. Devoured of rations, I try sipping water constantly to fill the growling space. My only comment to control A boiling temper is A smile, when A fat motorist squeaks to A right hand stop. With beady pig eyes over his double chin, and from across the highway he yells out.

"How far U going?"

"Newfoundland."

"Oh, U only have A few fifteen miles to the café. What U make A day, fifty, sixty miles?"

"Sir, the strength between sun up and sun down."

Montreal River Harbour, lots of stocked up food: bully beef, cheese, sweet bread, pure chocolate, raisin and dried apricots in yellow gold sections. Feet draggling in Pancake Bay Café. I'm restored with natural sinew, among the unworded descriptive carving of the breathtaking north shore road.

Sunday, June supper, after one of the most restful happenings of my water-loving life, I'm into the Norwegian Sauna steam bath, sitting on A perch-like board above the hot rock fireplace. Splattering the odd can of water on the rock grate below. It sends A penetrating heat steam through my blood body. The Jorgensen home on Mamainie Harbour bank holds the preciousness of Lake Superior hospitality. Too much, are the cabbage rolls with cheese and homemade wine to melt in your mouth? My body with toes to feel, where the steam bath joins heaven's ecstasy.

"Aaah, my kind people; I thank U from the heart's bottom, it is all I have to offer."

"We appreciate your company, A welcome guest U are at our home Hank. Here's A small parcel of smoked trout and herring to nibble between meals."

"Thanks, Harold, goodbye."

"Good luck Hank."

June nineteenth: In scalded foot walking pity, I grind my teeth in needle-emptied pain. Rats, I'm perked like stimulant coffee, standing at mid-day blaze in A green field park, at the base of A tall seven-foot monument. Monday, satisfied and happy. Horray! U good burnt feet, U have carried me here, halfway 2430 miles. I raise the squirt goatskin high, as sweet wine drips on face and lips. Few tourist move away as the charge of madness has been placed on me. I dance around in a happy cloud. From Victoria to St. John's, halfway! "Halfway!" I walk slowly to the backfield brook to sleep away the hot day sun under large maples, I'm delightfully-happy, and the crowd stares on.

Walking into A cool evening breeze, I prepare for A late night's walk of comfort. Now farewell to the last of my rain-bowed "Journée" and the sliver-sprinkle of Batchawana Bay. Black bank cloud obscures the heavens west; I see the flashing cut before the distant barrel roll-rumble. The night walks on, and cool Lake South breeze sprinkles the living nature. Even in the night, one senses the advance growth of the solution latitude. On a high wet dripping bush bank, I sleep through thunder fright. The blinding flares paint with bright colors on the yellow nylon pupper. The only chance for sleep is in the clear morning wind. I damp drag my cargo to the approaching city with five dollars for food, and A hope to find work here at Sault Ste. Marie.

For A journey that kisses
I wish I were fed,
The frogs in the pond
and flies in my bed.

Chapter 8

OPERATION DESPERATION....

I'm caressed in a pure green rain-washed morning, after a hard night bargaining with the Lock City hotel manager, for a bread-winning room. I will play for entertainment during three fifteen-minute band stops. The hustle job finding has a June heat wave and U.I.C. office place me on appointment two days from now. I burn the street from each garage, store, factory and dirty metal building without success. In the early evening sun, I sprawl on the lock bank park, watching and Algoma Steel ship rise on back fount water. Slowly the expansive bulk eases through the man-made channel; the distant stern-deck-pole waves A maple leaf flag, a profile rounding Sugar island.

My second night on stage, while playing to the roughest audience in town, and preparing for the last band stop, all hell breaks loose.

"Sir, I can't go out there, there's A bad fight on."

"Look, U got A three dollar room, so go out there and sing, spit or do anything, but quiet them down."

The fight is between me and the stage, how can I cross? I proceed in defense of the crash-gling glass bottles; I duck on the sheltered south side of the bar and dodge out the exit door. Strolling up-town for coffee, guitar slung over shoulder, the pub battle rages on.

I return to my room disturbed, and then find that A light hand of the hotel manager has stolen my blues mouth organ. Swallow the reeds in your craw, for my door was locked. My angry thoughts are soaring: Some people are less than kind. Crash, crash, someone is knocking.

"Well, what do U have to say Walker?"

"Say what?"

"Look fella, U didn't make the appearance, and that's five bucks for the room,"

"Sir, it was impossible, U know it."

"Look, don't give me that crap, bums like U have to pay five bucks or get out."

"I don't have the money, and what about the thirty minutes I played this evening?"

"U got one hour to get out, fella."

"Did U break into my room and take my harp?"

"Yes, I, paid for that mouth organ, and U were to play for A week. Get the hell out of here."

In the early morning mist of the bare streets and blue lights of hanging lamppost trees, I'm deprived among the destitute of A turbulent industrial life. The City Police search and check my belongings, for vagrancy is habitual in this water-lock city. I'm embracing the early morning stamina of sol's rays on the City Hall bench. The discouraging tears are A face wash, and I'm waiting empty and alone as if each city dweller spit and shut his door on my fingers. God I'm tired, better stand up and walk, try, look, anything. B-pitiful B-bothered, B-hungry or B-starved; I'm cradled among the agony of vultures. Joe explained hunger with cancer; this worries me when richness is abundant. Throw away my whole shot, nobody really believes me that I, just me, would walk this far. I believe my determination, and yet, how far will I walk from here?

Young MacDougall is standing at the counter when I approach car wash attendant for A job.

"Look fella, U couldn't buy A job, that's how slack this town is locked."

"Hi Hank, I'm Daniel MacDougall."

"Please to meet U."

"You're having a rough time finding A job? Now A friend and I have A pad, you're welcome to stay."

"Thanks."

The search goes on until my brother is the only alternative to my stomach growling. God bless brothers who answer their phones. I'm in the Sault, and he's South in that city-smog of Toronto. A long pause, dingo, operator, could U dial this number?

"Vic U old buddy, how's your money stashed up? Could U send me thirty to reach Sudbury from this hellhole? Lovely, lovely, tomorrow evening."

Early morning June twenty-third: Combed up and washed at Daniels room, I pull the final straw on job finding to the Centennial Replica Trading Post, for a "Coureurs de bois", they want.

"Who may I see for the acting Coureurs job?"

"U would have to meet with the Chamber of Commerce."

"Thank U"

I return from the river locks to the Town Hall Office. "I present U, Gresolon Du Luth, Nicolet or Lamotte Cadillac." There is always A great pause before the drawled refusal, but not A definite no; A run around from office to clerk, and my experience or hardship does not count. An intrepid fellow needs no introduction, but my idea is cast on the waves, I turn on calloused feet and enter the fresh day of A twilight summer, waiting till evening for the money, then mornings leave. On the park grass, I read the journal inscription the two hundredth times.

Never give up! IF adversity presses, providence wiscly has mingled the cup, and the best counsel, in all your distresses, is the stout watchword of "Never give up."

Encouraging phrase from:

Lucky, Lynda

And Boys.

Towards the East, where I may wake in happy fields, I leave this Saturday morning. Twenty-five dollars and thirteen cents to jingle loud, and one pair of new socks and boots reshod. I walk past to glare at the Lock City Hotel manager. Maybe I should pity him, enclosed in his liquor brawl room. My hair is chopped in A gouge; the lights are green, and the gray-moist wind-clouds blow the desolation from my mind. I follow the wind driven Lake Forest, tune – whistling on Echo Bay, "Never give up."

Beyond the scene
Man's mind scream
The spat withered dream

Chapter 9

A JOB OF WORK....

It is out I crawl from the bush of spruce, fly bitten and growling after A thunder flashing night of turbulence. On such A twenty-fifth sunny Sunday, I would stretch a mile but have to return walking. The freshness after the warm showery night, with needles hanging and tingling with silver rain specks, calms the mind's anxiety on a withered wooded ledge. A morning of breath freshness, I hoist the right pack strap pad to the bruised shoulder, slip the arm through, and tighten the Dutch strap to the fourth hole.

Two cheerful hours have whizzed by in the morning sun. The summer depth increases with each stride south, and I slowly forget about the Sault of Marie. I am encouraged and invited to visit the maple-flush-smell of St. Joseph Island. The white cap-licking waves soak my burning feet before I cross the quarter mile ferry trek. It's A three-mile journey from the highway through biting flies, frog-croaking swamp, to the channel float ride. One mile inside the maple leaf wind forest, the sunrays is peeking through trembling leaves. The Sportsmen Café holds out an afternoon of excitement for the highway-walker. Most of the island people are to visit me in their warm friendly manner on this water forest island. It's A fresh sturgeon steak dinner, coleslaw, vegetables and A milkshake.

"Thanks, Ryan."

Hank, "Eat and B merry we have the spare room ready. I'm A poet, who knows it?"

"Oh! What A pretty tidy room and A bed. You're very kind."

The intensity, like fire, has reached my feet, as the summer's heat-wave hits the burning green land. The dragonfly zings his penetrating droning song along the highway bush, and the smothering wave hits me like A flaming furnace. Cute chicks and breakfast, I'm trying to relieve blue emptiness, but it's like talking to A fish, A realistic wide-eyed stare and the question of, "Is he mad?" I clamp up, not to catch flies.

In the heat, June twenty-seventh mid-day, I unstrap the fifty-pound pack and snuggle in the tent under A large sky maple flush. So bitter sweet the taste of wild ripe strawberries; the handful I suck-melt and look for more. The hell-burnt heat has delayed me twelve hours from an appointed invitation at Iron Bridge High School. Walking through the night's fog to cool my body tissues, I arrive at witch hour, having midnight toast to wink love-bead smiles at A sparkly-eyed blond, serving black coffee. Committing A destructive balance by wake walking through the night, when rest is so essential, I find my body forced beyond agony. It's cloudy over the Blind River day-hours, trying iron gut-coffee to wake.

I arrive at Centennial Project Mercury, executed by the Signal Army Corps.

"What's the tower and tent hook-up on the roadside mean?"

"It's A cross country message, relayed from numerous stations from Victoria to St John's."

"How long are U here for?"

"Soon as the message is delivered. Would U like to try Army rations?"

"Great, thanks."

I walk to the adjoining park, exhausted after my night's duration. I pitch the tent and fall inside to smother in the burning-pic that may drive the "no-see-'em" flies to A death crash. B-gone with your stingers. My amount of rest reaches a chaotic end, when A busload of young school kids emerges on this little corner of my world. Crashing the under-brush, yelling war whoops and tossing sticks and dried roots, rocks and cans at my tent, I bail out. Hey, what the hell do U kids think you're doing? They scatter to the "Nun" driven bus. I grumble while packing; I'm thinking Hank is going to miss the quiet North.

I meet A three party canoe paddlers of pretty Thessalian girls, paddling from Matinenda Lake to Lauzon Lake, and we smile in comparison of experiences. I view A home-bakery West of Spragge; I bought two loaves of long round French bread, good with honey. The blue-turned-gray heavens break, raining like the Serpent Falls on green moss rocks, splatting and spitting on my back running cold and chafing my legs. I sneak for night's lodging into an abandoned car by a fly-festered bush swamp. The windows are shut; I burn the pic and huddle to sleep, wrapped in my bag.

Over I roll, grasp the neck, haul the body over the front seat, and pluck the old dusty chafed Gibson guitar to a droll song, singing among these void woods in the morning fog. I eat A wild strawberry breakfast while smashing with my left hand, the sticky biting flies. Wild crazy drivers burn the highway black; no wonder this Southern 17 road sees no wild life. Two British cyclists curse the weather, its heat, and the Canadian motorists for nearly running them over on a dozen occasions.

Special date! July first, and most wheel-flying families head towards Expo Montreal. There are swarms of bumper-to-bumper cars like A city jam in the early two-hand sunrise. Each stride-step is a promise for a "job of work" at the Sudbury, Nickel City. It's Saturday morning, three hands of sun, when I round the hilltop and look below to the branch-off road to Espanola and Manitoulin Island ferry. Oh God! In the distant view, A cream-colored car that whirled by me A minute ago, hauls to pass A Gray Hound climbing the long grade. The car charges headlong into the descending transport. The impact-smash arrives to my ears like seconds after the structure of the fenders, bonnet, windows, and wheels, fly, then disintegrate into the rolling dust of black smoke payment. When arriving at the ashes on the suicidal mound, the grass is wet with dew, and blood flows down the center white line of the blacktop. There are many bodies covered with gray blankets. The torn smell pukes my body. I sneak on, away from the gathered crowd, praying that my words mean something; very young was that family.

The gathered dairy herd in tall coarse clover red fields are trampling, too full to graze. I rest beyond the pasture field on A new cut swath. Oh the sweet smell, yet my mind visions those highway morning corpses.

Most campers rush for sitting room shelter as the black silence is cut by crash and bolt. I had A free shower here last night and camped close to the park. Running, oblivious from lightning, and camping gear bundled under arms, I stretch the hundred yard dash to the shelter. Among the Northern shield, the blazing thunder rolls loudly, following lakes and boulder timber slopes.

Natures cool fresh West wind blows sweet summers youth through the valley forest, after the last vicious thunder squall. The sun beams red one hand high, then pushing miles further, I finally arrive for A late breakfast. I'm famished as I enter the white Rose Garage Café, six miles East of Whitefish.

"I would like bacon and eggs, toast and A milkshake please."

"Thank U."

I better ask the proprietor for the washroom key.

"Look fella, your not good for my business, so grab your rags and move."

"Well Sir, I have my breakfast ordered."

"There's tourists in here all day, U haven't shaven for A week."

"I've got money for my breakfast and I'm starved."

"U better move, just go on, grab your things and go."

I stagger on Eastward Highway towards Sudbury, exhausted, hungry and dry from lack of nutrition. The summers greenness disappears in the approaching smog silt city. There's A barren rock-pile higher then most rolling hills, with A huge ceramic nickle screwed against the gray rising filth of the plant smelters. I order four burgers at the Nickle Burger stand and I'm crowded by two radio announcers who sit waiting for the immense appetite to B stuffed. The announcers are interested in my adventure, for many envision such a challenge.

Up and horray! Everybody is standing and lung yelling at the soccer field. I trudge pass the park to the down town Y.M.C.A., that continues A mile in length. Disappointed at the "Y," I head off for the Sally Ann. Found the helpers home around dusty brick block buildings, and my luck like an Irishman, I find an abandoned house fenced off for demolition. I have coffee in A near-by restaurant, and sneek in the shabby old house after dark to sleep the night with rats; drip-drop rain, and noisy are the drunks that climb the fences.

Monday morning for A "job of work" in July rain. The U.I.C. office, has no casual job. I walk the streets after checking back-pack at Y.M.C.A. for the days care. The moisture hung smog follows at eye level, never washing the dead grass in A city of permanent stains. "Tis late afternoon me boy, and to the Red Spoon junk and demolition camp I go. I follow Larry, A Newfoundlander I met up town, who lines me up with A buck thirty per hour demolition job. Jews and brothers are the bosses, and I work tomorrow!

Two days later, I find A board and room home, and the grinding days turn slowly. I gather ten dollars on an invitation to sing between band stops at the Casino Club Hall, which brings with advertisement A packed house. Thankful for the ten dollars, I pass the "bill" to the landlady and then skip-hop with Miss Wilson, my only joy in this lonely grey city. My small choking room bunk, away from my outdoor home of wild bird's call and an elegant dash of the fawn, is convenient.

Brother Vic and four other friends arrive from Toronto on Saturday for A visit. I am relieved from work at noonday sun, and join the boys at the rocky beach, watching the bathing sweets and eating pizza pie. Explaining my purpose, and enduring the journey of fully walking the cities and highway, is ridiculous in their minds. They fill with brew, and I try to B – A gracious host.

I'm buying A new wrap-around-sheet at mid-day break; the other canvas with rubber wrap is completely rotted out from the damp winds and rains I have experienced.

Such an evening that tarry on, singing my time away on boarding house steps, and strumming my guitar with Jackson, A Jamaican friend. I call on the mine and Mill Hall on Regent Street, and I'm

111

circled with name-dropping students and A Phys-Ed teacher who tries for no reason in my comprehension, to impress me. To hell with whatever you have to prove. I waited for the mail, and got A letter from home. I stand in front of a black bare city, thinking of the beauty I held last summer in 1966. My mind's recollection; A climb in the Kokanee glaciers, or old Mount Levana in the Purcell Range. That was grand, the smell of the ripe green and September flowers, the expectation for love to blossom from within the mountain angel's throne.

July twelfth: With A yawning face-wash and teeth brushed, I struggle towards the breakfast hash house, complaining to the red breast robin about his territorial call. "No cash, no fun, my clothes are tattered and boots are worn." It's the last workday and breakfast is good with A slow, sweaty day, tearing down boards from this old house. Smashing dust mortared walls with A crew of mixed race characters in their cool formations, are like the city dwellers who dare any outside friendliness to enter their closed circle. Morris the bull back newfy, in his brown tanned muscles with dust and sweat streaking his skin, does lots of whistling at the few cuties that pass along the street, three stories below. Washing the dust from the tangled mopped, chopped head before A stained and cracked sink, the seventy-dollar cheque is perched on the glass shelf. Aaah! Tis the food I'll buy, and the feet that will walk. That phony black-haired boy-escort-friend of Catherine's fumbled up the whole evening, for I had to fight or move on down the highway. I pray that the land with the forest-green summer will not B as dead as the smoke surrounding me here.

> *Before I lay this night at rest*
> *On bails of clover, my head is A test,*
> *I'll join the sweet lone-birds of nest*
> *God is all and there I rest.*

Chapter 10

LONESOME HIGHEWAY BLUES....

Revenge, revenge, what U're looking for I can't give. The smoked choked city is among the bare bouldered granite below my left shoulder gaze, and each bend is entering the green and wild. There's A group of stick-boys holding A pow-wow in front of the abandoned barn to the highway's left.

"Hey, U guys, stop your rock pelting."

"U nutty bum, get the hell out of here."

Slingshots spring A burning sting to my left leg, but I'm three quarter protected behind the pack, dashing clumsily down the road.

The sun holds steady one hand high above the valley gorge spruce, and I fill McQuack with seeping black tea. I stand naked, sprawled with one long toe foot on separate rocks in the pure cold mountain stream, soaping the perspiration to the croaking frogs, "They'll change voices." Those bloodlust flies; if I build A green branch smoke fire, I may advance the theory of suffocation; they or I have got to go. Nothing like steeped black tea when you're tired. Believe it, A week away from the highway softens my fitness. This fur-branch mattress separates my throbbing heart from the damp truth of the clay, to which someday I will return. I join both hands holding my head as A pillow. Could it B the clicking of the wristwatch below the surface Pacific, where I tossed its tinkle body in the ocean? Time will follow nature, and I'm always hours behind the mad rush traffic. The silent, lonely gurgling moss-rock-stream ticks my time of happiness, and A different style of life that I have chosen, endures and keeps the sweet dreams lull.

Night black, stage left, up and bouncing the rocky surface and peeled up like A banana with A blunt stop, the crash charges on. I'm choked in this straight jacket tent, water gargling down my back. I slowly poke one arm through the tangled zippered flap, half wet and bruised. Frightened, I crawl from destruction's path, lifting my tent from the watered streambed. It's A moose track! A speeded bull. He got spooked from the highway night and charged over the thicket bank, knotting my tent rope with him. Luckily the small rope broke. Calm down Hank; am I ever shaky? I have found dry branches and the match lights quickly. I'm lucky the guitar wasn't splintered, but many character marks chip it's body.

The large crystal raindrops washing the barren streets, wake the sleeping dew-worm-catcher who hops stiffly to his next squirming gulp. On three hands of sun early evening, I'm scared-sweating as four leather-vested girls squeal to A stop in A hopped-up Ford. It's a living nightmare but it's day-bright. I'm cold-shivering with the thought that girls could bet, and my life is at stake like an animal of blood and flesh. Held with a pocket knife at my throat, the money I have none, and their dissolution is angered. An approaching car saves my life; he squeal-stops and the "girl gang" leaves.

From Prince George, A couple, Joe and Peggy are musically touring Canada. Here inside the Sturgeon Falls Hotel. I join the Saturday matinee.

Sweet warm rain, such is beauty; the Nipissing Lake bends away from the highway noise, for miles before reaching North Bay. There's A shack on the rocky mold, A tall scrawny figure, arm beckoning to join him.

"What are U lugging?"

"I'm Hank."

"Well yes! I know about U, have A seat."

I sit in his sunk out, cross flapped rocking chair, on the small veranda under A large washing tub, hung by A nail on the shack wall. Tea is good while the rain drips from the roof. The hippie memories of Prince George's days, of preparing this walk in the twenty odd below weather, was like a dream. My body is ripe physically, but mentally tortured with endurance and loneliness.

"Go on young man, do what U must."

"Cherrio Jack."

"Safe journey Hank."

There are small flowers with crimson blooms in the hearts of the young, and tenderly they follow me on the sunny Sunday entry to

North Bay. We sit about the laundromat telling stories; big bass, long swims and canoe rides.

The sickly heat of the July eighteenth wave turns my stomach with headaches. I cool in the murky water of a Mattawa stream and join the Walkers for A spaghetti chicken supper. The Salvation Army Captain with his wife and family drive North with their trailer. I follow the Valley East; the Laurentian rolling green, meets the blue from the Mattawa River on the Quebec spruce and willow bank.

Late the following day, with the heavens erupting in drenching rains, I finally top the padded green hills. Around the bend flat valley river, sits Deux Rivieres. Such a rare and tender steak, touching the grill sizzling; choice cut by A soft-spoken French cook.

Each day passes like tedious hours and I mother-love each step, as I tighten the coureur strap. The valley is beautiful and the season is young. The July mist is blowing from the turbine gate-fall where the electric turbines generate these nearby prosperous cities. I meander, slowly slipping up the green-mossed rocks to A poplar grove ledge. It overlooks both highway and man-made dam only feet below in the swirling white foam rise. A rainbow of many colours from the penetrating red-gleam sun, descends behind the West Laurentian green slopes.

At "Rapids des Joachims," I stand in rolling laughter by A Volkswagen bug who barrels head-long into the ass end of A highway bull moose. The creature flips up and lands solidly on the poor bug's back, smashing the top shell to seat level. Such A graceful beast! It shakes its carcass from the roof hood, blood dripping from its foggy acquaintance with the Volkswagen. The long fast, grace full moose strides crashes in the young spruce. The driver red-faced, seated in his wrecked bug, raises A choking abusive rot-gut lingo from his sealed up car. I extend my five pound number 8½ foot through the back window. Prying the tin bulge up, I drag the cursing occupant from the car, and leave in A hurry from the Deep River Valley heat.

As the persistent infernal heat glows the black oil tar-top highway, elusion waves arise in the distant mirage. I record its temperature off 105°, reflecting from the choking ebony road. I hold up from mid-day, till three hands before sun down. The scorching rays have cured the swathed hay fields and over ripened the sweet wild berries. Even the oats and wheat fields are turning yellow; I notice the crowding cattle under A small shaded grove; the flies and heat are A torturing hell.

Chalk River before sun down, and now midnight, I'm inside A Petawawa café. In A trance of my elusive dream, the inferno has allowed me no rest, and my feet stumble on through the night trying to cover miles. Glaring empty into this filmed brown mug of coffee, I scratch out these words: "Clear hot blue river, and under a tree the day will keep." Night frog catches the fly he eats, I wither on through the heat, waiting for the cool rain to soak my feet and hair, then run down my back. Who cares about Chafe?

Young dreams of melancholy road, and double feeling of cool loneliness, I pound on towards Pembroke, Ontario. The early camouflaging mist, covers all but my mind that wanders far in the dreams of A schoolboy, gum chewing and sucking his eraser tipped pencil, with elbows in meditation position. The stars are the limit and I continue the walk with a feeling of confidence, that I will cross this vast Continent, I hear the mocking laughter of many that I have shared this dream with.

His bulk comes barging through the fog, and I am safe on the gravel shoulder. Screaming of air brakes and rubber burning, my night quietness is shattered with glare.

"Hey!" "What is your big idea?"

"Walking across Canada; have to night-walk because of the heat."

"Well, I'll B damned!" "I thought coming through the fog U were A moose or cow." "Good luck."

"Thanks, cheerio."

Voom doom, and the fog closes in behind the night rider.

Seven thirty breakfast, July twenty-second, and temperature is in the eighties. Pembroke streets are burnt, lonely and quiet, and tourist highway traffic shoppers are looking for A city trademark souvenir. I move on through the riverbank town, and converse with A pretty miss radio announcer. I study the mud-oil Ottawa River bank for A camp location; I have to crash. I've got sixty miles covered on three hours of sleep!

Head into the sun, young man, where victory is sweet. I find my courage like a magnet star where Champlain fought on this very spot in 1603. That was A very good year of escape and adventure in this birthright Country; like A "coureur de bois" ... "huzza, huzza, pour le pays sauvage." The wild birds sing from the vanishing days of man's entitled freedom.

Late Sunday evening, I slowly consume A small toasted cheese sandwich; my first stable food to steady the innards, for the heat and exhaustion have soured my stomach. I feel better with sun-down cooling and Renfrew is behind me. The traffic rolls heavy, and then A black Thunderbird pulls to the opposite gravel shoulder.

"Hi!"

"Good evening Mam."

"Do U mind telling me what U are doing?"

I squint across the hazy road, cranky and tired in the early evening dusk, and look upon A dark shaded woman who penetrates with A strong, sharp voice.

"I'm walking the Continent from Victoria to St. Johns."

I explain my purpose and challenge.

"U didn't really walk all the way from Victoria, B.C. to here?"

"Look lady, you're calling me A liar after I have explained to U for ten minutes, and this road has taken me six months to reach here." "U are wasting my precious time, good evening."

"I didn't mean to insult U; do U know who I am?"

"No, and I don't care."

"I'm Secretary Of State."

"Oh yes! "Secretary of State." I could crawl under A culvert if there was one handy."

"Call my office when U arrive in Ottawa, I'll see that U will find A job." "Good luck."

"Cherrio."

Darkness is upon the many dairy herd shadows that moos and sniffs along the elm edged field. I turn left following A dirt road up over one of many low rolling hills, that causes the beauty of the valley to "tableau" in colorful outline. I stake and tie up my tent A quarter mile from the Highway 17 noise. Calm and rest, I must have. The lightning glows inside the tent upon pain of burning eyes, and then quietness lulls in the early morning dawn.

Finally, in the sun, waking sheepishly, I penetrate the partly unzipped flap; with elbows extended and I on four crawlers, I stare head-on upon A gray mortared gravestone. McArthur, 1849 to 1901.

Oh hell, if I would have known that the lump under my back was that
A grave stiff, I would've steered clear or shot out of here last night.

Warm South-west wind meets the cloud rising North, and over the
Ottawa Valley meadows the thunder rain seeps warmly and heaven
glows. With careful precaution, I fold my tiny portable home, drink
two raw eggs with an orange and milk, then two hard tack cookies. I
feel happy and rested on "entry" into Canada's Capital, Ottawa.

Green yellow flame with burnt on feet
Moose tracks, thunder upon my sleep,
Angelic corps of bearded stiffs
When I turn up on natures cliff.

No singing on Mall?

By Mike McDermott
Citizen Staff Writer

Hank Gallant, the British Columbia folk singer walking across Canada as a Centennial project, nearly stumbled Thursday night.

He tried to sing on the Mall.

Gallant, who has walked more than 2,850 miles since he left Victoria's Beacon Hill Park Feb. 6, has been welcomed in dozens of villages, towns and major cities along his route to St. John's, Nfld.

But he bombed in Canada's capital.

The 24-year-old former fisherman from Tignish, P.E.I., strode into Ottawa late Wednesday unaware of the delicate Mall problem between civic authorities and the city's young hippies.

The Mall has become a gathering spot for Ottawa teen-agers, and city police are a little sensitive about any excitement which may occur on it.

The sight of a lean, bespectacled guitarist, complete with faded baseball cap and mouth-organ singing on the Mall last night was more than the two policemen on duty could take.

"Off," said the policemen.

After a short argument which got him nowhere, Gallant left the Mall and returned several minutes later with a letter of introduction from the 1967 Exhibition Association, co-sponsors of Expo 67 and Centennial celebrations.

"Off," repeated the unimpressed policemen.

After another short argument, the policemen invited Gallant to go for a ride to the police station "to get things straightened out."

"I can't do that," said the marathon walker, "I haven't been in a car since I left Victoria and I don't plan to get into one now."

"Well I certainly don't plan to walk to the police station," replied one of the constables.

At one point, the confused policemen decided to let the young hiker sing but seconds later, with the arrival of another policeman, changed their minds.

Hank picked up his guitar and strode off to the Waller Street Police station seeking permission to sing on the Mall.

But the police referred him to the Mall Authority and Hank, a little weary of Ottawa's red tape, thinks he might just forget the whole thing.

"If I've got to run all over town just to get permission to sing the same songs I've sung in every other place I've been in, I think I'll just forget it," he said.

"I've never had anything like this happen to me before, it's incredible.

"I'm walking across Canada and singing songs I've written about Canada as a Centennial project. The only place I've had any trouble is in the capital of Canada."

When Gallant passed through Cranbrook, B.C., on the first leg of his journey, the town turned out in the hundreds to welcome him and he was treated to his favorite meal, spaghetti and chicken, before continuing his trip.

"When I went through Fort Macleod it was 38 degrees below zero but the people still turned out.

"It isn't always like that though," he said, "I was thrown out of a restaurant just outside Sudbury a few weeks ago because the owner said I was scaring the tourists away. That was on July 2, the day after Canada's birthday.

About singing on the Mall tonight?

He doesn't know.

Nobody knows.

Chapter 11

WE DON'T ALLOW NO GUITAR
PLAYING HERE....

To the left spears Parliament Hill, mingled with various shades of trees, monuments, fountains and lawn seated people, A busy hour and the sun hides behind the tall black building central office, of white collar civil servants. I baffle with the warm wind and empty stares from the many solemn glares that I receive while walking through Spark Street Mall. My sunburnt face and two weeks of hard straight bleached beard is an appearance to discern. Received two letters; one from Sis, and five dollars enclosed in Mother's envelope. I'm on easy street, five dollars and thirty-seven cents! On returning to the Sparking Mall, I inquire which direction for the "Y". A group of longhaired youths directs me four blocks into City Centre. I'm rushed by two Policemen who drag me off through an alley, to A waiting paddy wagon.

"Hey! What's the big idea?"

"Look fella, we want U down at Head Quarters."

"What did I do?"

"You're one of them long haired jerks who have been putting suds in the fountain. We got orders to run U bastards off the Mall."

Police brutality, police injustice; the first shaking crowd gathers. Most people recognize the villain through his news coverage.

"Look officer, could U allow me to walk to the Police Station?"

"Who in the hell do U think you're joking?"

"But Sir, to ride in any form of vehicle will defeat my purpose."

"Look U, if U are who U say, with all that walking this drive won't hurt."

"One of U officers can walk with me, and the other can follow in the wagon."

"B hell if I will walk down to the Station with U. Okay, I yet think you're mad, we'll lead the way."

Two Johnny-on-the spot reporters follow the scene of the villain, as I constantly hurdle the high and clutch the guitar neck firmly; I hop along to the Police Station. Seated, I'm waiting for the Sergeant to call my name from inside A paneled door office.

"Hank Gallant, this way."

Oh oh, what will happen? Better, leave my pack and guitar. Inside, behind A large mahogany desk, sits the steel jawed, raw boned, and black eye browed book thrower. I'm scared skinny; if he yells I'll wet my pants. A quick call to the "Secretary of State" and my problem is solved.

"U can go, but remember, no guitar playing on the Mall."

"No Sir, I didn't know, but U won't catch me there again."

The piped-in music is mellow on the sparkling Mall morning. I'm A victim of rage and fury between City Aldermen, the Centennial Committee, and the flashing news coverage that discovers the Century Committee is not recognizing my walk project. I'm censored and disdained among cold views. I thumb soberly through A notebook, and find the Walkers number of the Salvation Army Captain who offers his full help. I have a trailer on wheels to reside in while working in Ottawa and A job at A speedy car wash. I leave the cold, unfriendly city where only hours ago, I had reached here in the good cheer of my Capital and was instantly caught up in the circumstances. Returning eight miles to the open country and Bells Corners, where each morning for seven continuous days, I pursue the five mile tromp to the city and the job of work. The recurrent daily walk keeps the muscles in shape from relaxation.

July thirty-first: While the wet moisture hangs dripping upon the bodied soldier elms, the red breast chirps and stiffly hops, looking for A watered out earthworm; maybe to feed her nested young. Song tunes, and much happy feeling, as I leave the dismal city behind for one more night of rest. A tall brunette, she stands waiting and wrapped in A pink robe, hiding her eyeball bikini, welcomes me.

"Hi, my name is Jill."

"Hi, very fine. I'm Hank."

126

"I know, read your coverage and saw U passing. "Would U like to come and join my Grandparents and I for supper?"

After this amiable sup with gracious strangers of the valley green, I feel happiness and bliss, that more are warmer than the loud that fuss. I momentarily forget the white collar stench of my Capital City.

For A Tuesday dip, I skip-hop across the dried lawn park. Many withered yellow leaves are gliding groundward and the heat wave burns on. Rounding the river bank. Jill leads the way following the small gravel water edge to the swimming area. Who's the bow-legged chicken to B in last? Recovering from the slimy water, I curiously observe A passing antique car rally with two 1909 Silver Cloud Royces, and A 1902 Dennis shiny-waxed in exhibition. The puking sewer water, "swim at your own risk", is desperately common on the Ottawa River.

Oh lady luck, shine your light on me in sky skip moments, and be happy with joy. The gathering is large in A pow-wow circle around an open yard barbecue. Mr. Walker aproned, with the help of his good friend Michael, deep fry the fish steaks. Tonight, the fields of green with the soft quiet canoe wake the river blue. Songs are mellow, and some flurried by the excellent time-handling of a tambourine beat. The evening blurs with happiness and the well-wishing words of A strong slap on the back for luck. I soak these feet in preparation for my resumed morning journey. Refusing A token gift this afternoon from the City council and Mayor, I'm asked to walk ten miles entering Ottawa to B presented with A goodwill gift, the end result of my treatment. His voice angered with tone when I said, "Sorry, Sir, I'm invited to dinner and wouldn't care to spoil my appetite. I'll wave the City farewell from the by-pass highway in the morning."

When the last bright yellow coal slowly turns gray and the tea cup tastes the last drop, the kids slide from their shyness and unwind with curious questions. The parents lug their children home with questions asking: "How many pairs of boots did U wear out so far Hank?"

So green
So blue
So true,
Push and haul
With life so small.
Hank.

WESTERNERS PRAISED

Hank cited many humorous incidents along his trip and praised people through the West for helping him. "Once, right at the top of a mountain, an Italian-Canadian family from Trail, B.C., brought me a spaghetti dinner. When I mintioned it during an interview on Cranbrook's radio station, a family nearby supplied me with another," Hank said.

"Another time a farmer, in an old truck, stopped and asked me where I was headed, I told him that I was walking across Canada and refused his offer of a two-mile ride. ther farmer stared at a near by tree for about 15 seconds then slowly turned his head towards me. He started at my feet and slowly studied me. Then, with no warning, he jerked the old truck forward and rattled away. That look he gave me was so funny that I had to remove my pack and rolled in the ditch laughing."

The pack he carries, weighing about 50 pounds, contains food, mainly canned, a harmonica, guitar, an extra pair of boots, and several other essential items.

What next? Hank is keeping a log on his daily travels and hopes to write a book. He also is considering returning to B.C. with a trek through the United States and, in 1969, is hoping to walk across Europe.

"I wanted to do this before I settled down," he said.

Hiker survives B.C. blizzard but
WANTED TO DIE IN PRAIRIE HEAT

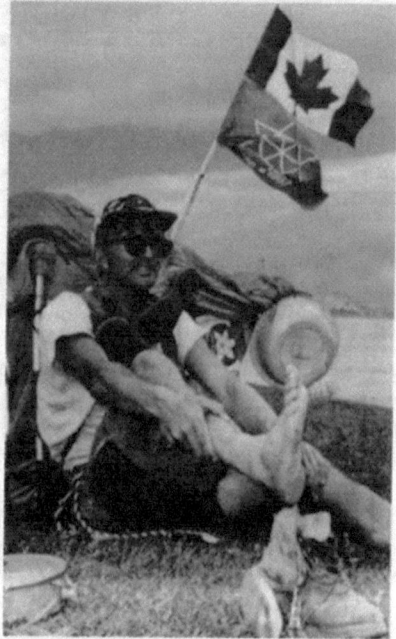

BOOTS AND BLIZZARDS:

Hank Gallant rests weary feet at Expo after his 3,000-mile trek from B.C. His story was of boots and blizzards, scorching sun and prairie pavements. Why did he do it? To remember Centenial year. "I'll never see it again."

129

Chapter 12

TO MONTREAL WITH ITCH.....

August fifth: A bright sol streamer morning, as I head East on Queensway by-pass, walking close to the guardrail, frightened of the speeding traffic. The "Walkers" packed me A lunch, and the cracker box dangles from its string among A knife and sash cord. This dodging traffic is bad, but I feel lifted on A pure white cloud. The road is dusty-dry with A promise of further clover fields. Bye-bye Jill, until we meet again; I wave goodbye to Ottawa with stone-formed block houses and black smokey barred windows. I wonder why friendship is exhausted in this cold-seated Capital City. I stride on following the River Ottawa.

The feel of cold water on stinging feet and twice A change of boots and socks. The fresh evening riverbank breeze is strong enough to keep the flies at a distance. Stretching out in the tent, shoulders leaning against the sleeping bag, I pluck the Gibson and drawl the blues harp, singing about the snake charm-walker.

Walking from Cumberland to Rockland is a good breakfast appetizer. The hills of inspired serenity have turned into an animated emerald. The farmland, at some point, is broken by willows entangled with thorns and green leaf mesh swamps. My hills are disappearing to the North-east.

With mind against matter, suggesting that reason of mind does not operate or is at ease when body muscles function constantly tire the mental concept. The determination theory forces me to do till I die on this distant walk.

I swallow A taste of cold deep well water which I collect from A "Voi-sine" farmer. His speedy dialect baffles me compared with my rolling Acadian accent.

"My River,"

"Why yes,"

"Notre Riviera ... And the papers show A warning not to swim in the Ottawa River because it has caused horrid food poisoning to humans lately."

For A century or two of progress without control-planning has contaminated our streams and lakes. My forefather the "coureur," Pierre explains, "has paddled lovingly without knowing that today A paddle may vanish when dipped in the stream. Have another drink of deep well water."

Alfred, Ontario, in its swamp thundering morning, I crawl out in tall grass, benevolently looking for weather signs. The name sounds different, with its population speaking French; Alfred rests sheepishly quiet from the wakening rains. I look feverishly tired with a slow swoop-sag in my walk and eyes. I drink gallons of water before dusk, and at Hawkesbury by-pass, the red itchy water blister-swellings are appearing on my back and legs, mostly in chafing locations. Darkness creeps over in shadowy form, waking the attack of the blood flies. I drive my newly cut tent stakes in an erect location on the bank of A pasture stream, lightly smudged with cow leavings. Bathing in quiet darkness, I cool with the soaping water flowing down my legs to tent mud-mingling toes. Yahoo and the flies I wash down the stream. Gathering dried elm branches from the corner field from uprooted trees, I use A lunch bag paper to light the hot flame for the green steeped tea; four cups. The bright blanket of stars A silhouette at fingertip reach. I rest against A trembling leaf poplar, a substantial giant. With troubled kidneys from cold ground sleeping, I may wet the sack.

The heat festered body looking for the warmth of sunrays, and I'm weakening with the thought of the day ahead. "God, it's poison ivy." Large water blisters in the crotch and on my back where I will torture with chafe. Two days back, I must have camped after dark in A patch.

This croak hatching crow with her shiny black feathered mate is fussing in the nearby bush, and old mamma stands beak and claw, ready to defend her nest. Looking East, I stand viewing the return of the now gathered neighboring flock, in a fight squawk to scare what is on the prowl.

Twelve miles and five hands of sun-up, with my bellowing rejoicing cry victory of 1445 miles, is the longest Province of my walk. I'm at the Quebec border toasting well water, seated, sewing the

"Ontario Leaf Cross" coat of arms crest. "Huzza, huzza pour la marche à pied", and victory will come in future months.

Finding A small bush pond to hide in cat tail rushes, I bath the water blistered cleavage throbbing skin. Ochre and warm is my first sunset in this new Province walk, and it's A grinding fifty-pound weight smashing the eroded ivy-water blisters. Camping alongside the railroad track, hiding under A willow bush fifteen or more miles from Montreal, I drink gallons of water and try to sleep with sweating chill blains.

"Montreal, ce matin". I'm in the bush hiding pink; my body is burning and stumbling onto the highway. Walking A mile to pass Dorian with A bottle of pink ivy solution while the mid-day sun glows blindly through A smoke screen above my head, I finally approach the Express way entering the city. Expos Police Patrol guides me over the concrete high rise road. Finally, after A hair raising journey through speeding Montreal traffic, I walk upon the Exposition parking ground. Viewing below with emotional happiness, I gaze upon the world globe of heritage display with angles upon the shape, exploding my stomach into tingles. Spread out arm's length in shouting voice, hurray, hurray, three thousand miles I've conquered and now on the steps of the world's culture fair.

With each step, I feel numbness in my body movement as I turn right from the "Place d'accueil" entry and escorted to the Administration Building.

"August the tenth: It has taken U all this time?" "Are U sure U have walked all the distance?" asked the English-speaking reporter.

With questions puncturing and ridiculed by the news media, the hours pass long with my fever very high. It's impractical to sit square solidly on my bottom with these large festering water blisters which burst and water sticking my clothes with pus. It's impossible to find A reasonable, if any, sleeping accommodation. The "Y" and youth hostels are filled; it's A crazy tourist over-run city. Sitting, burning with fever, I'm canted on one elbow position waiting for my ten A.M. appointment dinner at the Canadian Pavilion. The leather chair at the Administration Building is my accommodation for the night. Oh God, the strength I need.

News has hit the morning paper as I savour coffee so very black and strong that A frog would choose it as his mud pond. Eager for the morning's appointment, the body stoops in a putty blob while I itch to view the World's Fair. Reaching the Canadian Pavilion, where the dinner appointment is due, the chills increase with weakness. My mind pivots with fever and turns rolling black in the Canadian Pavilion, and how very sick my body cries. "I can't sit to eat; can I eat and stand?" "Garçon," the waiter brings the wine samples, and I choose. I taste it, but all I see is pink, or is it orange? After dinner and A sip of wine, I am led to the St. Johns Ambulance Post, where A doctor checks and has me rushed to the Island Hill General. I remember the tall trees and flat leaf scope shade; there is A large roll snake ball bouncing towards me, and I can't move, for the frightening fever comes again.

On Sunday gleam rays, I gaze from A August twelfth hospital window. Below St. Catherine and Dorchester Streets, is a turmoil of an exceeding view population. Beyond the high square block window, rising like A sky hook hanging, A blimp sails lightly on the Sunday breeze with flags and banners waving in the heavens blue. "Welcome, welcome to Expo". I whisper quietly under my breath, I feel defeated, for the ambulance ride has broken the spirit purpose. I regard the view, itching and wondering how long will I B in exile.

The gentle care of A smiling physician has treated me with pills and needles for my festered body. "Well Hank, U are patched quickly as possible for the road. Treat your sores with this lotion and wash daily and change clothes: U are discharged from the Hospital this afternoon."

August hot, five hands sun with the choking silence smog dust blue, I slowly return gently walking bow-legged. I enter in the tangled jungle zoo life with no mail and no money from the Income Taxation Office. I crash out in Tony's apartment, A friend from Vancouver. I'm waiting for morning and the smiles from the bubbly Hostess to escort me in the completion of my day tour, delayed by the itchy ivy predicament.

"Good morning sunshine, ain't gonna rain no more." I pull out from other crashed-out friends, with sleeping bag sweaty and sticky. After wash up, brush and comb, I leave for the final tour of Expo, A remembered day in Montreal.

Miss Monique, U are so lovely; what A sunshine smile walking with U from the Administration Building. We follow the River Harbour to visit the Blue Nose replica.

"U would prefer to ride the railcars entering onto the Islands Expo?"

"No, Monsieur Gallant, I don't mind walking this pretty morning."

We cross the river canals to the Islands of Man and His World, where "Le Labyrinth" is our first entertainment. By passing the large lineup with our V.I.P. pass cards, Britain, Czechoslovakia, U.S.S.R. and Mexico Pavilion, we gather close to where A group of churros play and sing in their native tongue. Monique so pretty in her smiles and blue uniforms with golden long hair. By A silent fountain on the bank of the canal, we escape the thousands of trampling viewers. Trinidad and Tobago Pavilion is on the left, and overhanging the water canal, the band chalet, with twenty steel drum musicians playing in blood-warming harmony, their rhythmic music to the world's finest dark rum.

The ivy-festered tour included seven cultured domes followed by an evening gathering. The pretty hostess with friends, Betsy Sue and others, sing the evening away on the Dorchester apartment steps. Worried man blues, worn out shoes on A Montreal August fifteenth smog humid evening.

To itch and bitch
To wine and dine
To love and smug.

Chapter 13

HABITANT HOSPITALITY....

The cool shower, it's A draining wash for my crying blisters. I lotion on the pink coating and pack my gear. For now, the streets have cooled in the early morning sunrise. Heading downtown St Catherines sidewalk turmoil, I threaten to walk abruptly with the triangle pack frame; A bump on the head if they don't move. There's A click-clunk marching sound from my new shod hiking boots.

High above the gray-water of St Lawrence River and crossing on Jacques Cartier Bridge, there is clear weather in the skies. Yonder, tinge globe roofs are among the few transplanted trees, as the people thick like hair, cover in swarms, the locations on both "Île Sainte-Hélène," and "Île Notre-Dame." The metro train rattles, and the canal boat chugs, carrying human cargo to the Isles of Man and His world. The contemplative watch of amusement grounds with big painted wheels, coaster cars and loads of thrilling rides now past below on the left. "Tête ou queue," on the approaching rail of the bridge, I sit flipping A quarter from my sole surviving forty dollars in the worn leather wallet. Quarter flips tails, and I take #3 Highway following the river scenery instead of #20 Highway inland.

Reaching Boucherville at four hands of sun, I realize that forgetting my water can on the bridge post miles back has now caused

A fluid shortage, and fever begins to burn my chafed body blisters. I call into A vendor store; the wine will help the pain, and maybe I'll forget the whole watery mess. In Verdatre, Que., before the red glow ball hides in the West hills, many long narrow green habitant fields are touching the milky-looking polluted river. Sipping the last of mid-sweet wine and hiding the bottle behind A thorn bush, I pass through A willow-edged green bank to the river rocks and sand beach. Counting the red-lighted port holes of this passing freight ship, I enjoy the quiet of the evening river breeze, pitching camp under an overhanging willow. I tie the front entrance high and the back rope on A perched tripod. Wading naked in slime-oily water to cool my festered body, I'm eighteen miles past Montreal's night-light-life. Happily, I convinced the doctor for early release from Montreal Hospital, and it's "great" to B under the sky quilt heavens on muddy river sand.

My days of struggling torment in slowly exceeding twenty miles are flat fresh hell. The people I meet are observant and warmly pleasant, especially when I try to talk the "Français." I dip in public pools, small streams and old St River, tossing back A daily bottle of Port, the red medium that dulls and kills the pain and brings to my mind A dilapidated song. There's A group of youngsters calling A welcome gesture to their private campground. With sundown in the cooling evening, we gather around A large log fire singing both languages and trading songs. Finally, I crawl with an excuse manner to A popular grove that overhangs A twenty-foot shale bank. I wonder after pitching A tent, could I B lucky like most "coureur" to paddle on drift quiet river? However, I have to portage the distant journey. Where did that Port bottle go? Here here, may U help me sleep with this agony.

Sorel for A quiet breakfast with fresh morning friendliness, and A "bonjour" waitress who serves with such poise and delicacy, places the cutlery with skilled ability. Ah! "Merci"; even if I stick to the leather upholstered chair! Motorists stop, asking many continual repetitive questions. "Are U frightened of terrorists or separatists? U fly high the Canadian and Confederation flags, why?" I close my sweating lashes behind black shades, nod A grin and walk on, exhausted in the ninety-degree temperature.

Saturday, August nineteenth: Waken in a dream sweat as clouds are rolling among my subconscious thoughts; I'm in A field of green clover smells, shrinking in scared hiding. The loud footsteps are crunching militantly toward my little yellow tent, and the saucer ship steps spread, waiting for an earthly capture. They reach carefully to miss nothing in one grasp black hair hand, and I scream in sweated pain at their pointed ears....

Early morning has floated the blue on a green dream, and by the mid-day sun, I enter Pierrevilles Indian Reserve in search of the chief and his prescribed herb medicine. In A plastic bag, one pound of dried mixture of herbs which Chief Charlie won't tell about but explains.

"U boil a quarter of these herbs in A pint of water, allow it to cool, then bathe the ivy blisters."

"How much, Chief?"

"One dollar."

"Thanks."

"All the best, for U need no handicap on the walk."

I peer into the platonic quiet night across this slow-moving seaward river and the yellow speck glow from the Habitant house window. Marie and Janette are camping ten yards upstream on the sod bank, hitch-hiking towards sunset. There's a peaceful allusive lull on the sod bank river as I gather small fire twigs so that we may relax in comfort. We sip from paper cups the green lemon tea and hot bun rolls pasted with honey. The supper is filling, so here's to spaghetti meatballs and sauce. Black clouds rolling East cool the rising wave temperature.

"We may have A wet day on the highway tomorrow Marie."

"Are U walking through the Gaspe"?

"No, I follow # 2 highway."

The Nicolet main streets are being sprinkled with A cool Northeast rain, with Sunday churchgoers splattering in their wrapped-around rain gear. I like the feel of soft heavenly water to wash the nights running pus clean, and the forenoon rest stops are wet and cool. There's A chill that runs my body during dinner of a hot chicken sandwich. I can't place the rain gear on because of the chafe, and I walk hard to keep warm. Sharp left sway towards St Laurent on Highway 3 at villa St Gregorian, the rain pours in sheets that soak the extra weight to pounds heavier. I shed the left shoulder strap and wheel right to catch the house pack lowering it gently. Ahh! Relief, one thousand pounds lighter.

The "ville" of St Angele de Laval has A dark mahogany painted pine board café, and nature's pure window-washer chills A cool feeling as I sit at A round table, cozy, sipping tea that warms but looks and taste like dishwater. Now the road is soggy with these water-loaded boots, and dark demons with troll eyes are peering from across the swirling river current on Trois-Rivieres town. A beacon light peeks in warning of the night's approach, and I'm pleased for the twenty and more miles that I have covered. This wayfarer nomad finds A wrecked car on the approach to the stock track. I change into comfortable, warm clothes and crawl into the back seat with the down bag; windows are good while the rain taps roof-tin like a rattling machine gun. "Christ was among the fishermen in A rainy boat; thanks for the warm clothes on the muddy watered ground."

High steps with swinging "fleur" skirt dancing of the joyful Habitant, wear bonnets off white and pink. Hard-working, down-to-earth, and checkered-shirted men are young in prime, and others wiser with the experience of age. Toes tap as I view these dances and open festivity.

I wake among the willow bank and thorns near Ste Antoine de Tilly; in the early morning, I harp droll and pluck twang my Gibson.

Who peers over the timothy hay bank? An old man and his son. Here goes, I'm on his land.

"Salut!"

"Entré."

"We come early for cutting the wheat in the upper field, but dew is heavy. We heard the music. My son Nicolas, he thinks it's radio, we both come see. U play song well. Nicolas, he plays music A bouche."

"Well, let's go."

When dust rises from the bare patch surrounded by willow and thorns, the old chap nudges his son to sneak home.

"Don't forget, enter the back laneway and inside the clay cellar behind that carrot bin"… "le vin".

Renewed vigor returns from the beet red fluid wine. Nicholas arrives, and the toast is high up, jug-A-lug, for the voyageur sips, and the wheat is untouched. The beets were good four years ago. Aah, bittersweet, and now the music swings in the habitant step, with Edmund dusting his lively sixty-year-old steps. Nicolas wails that droll harp back, both eyes shut in a trance, and I strum my thumb to A blister. Old Sol rises higher in the sky, and gaiety flies the clouds with A steamship whistleblowing.

"Edmund, U sneak. Have U gone crazy with the wheat ready for mowing?"

Then she shrieks in French for A good fifteen minutes. The jug is passed.

"Here, fill your wineskin; sorry Henri for the abrupt end to our lively outing."

I stagger on down the lane-way, not feeling the burnt chafe crotch, only the cold stare of the brown fiery-eyed farmer's wife.

Serene miles are captured in the happiest of smiles, with bubbly-bubbly feeling, stumbling through clover meadow. I follow the fence and into the mud milky river as I sit splashing the pus running down in old river sand. The private property signs and beware of dogs edges me to the highway. West heaven dusk turns ocher, and the cooling wind bids an industrial smoke whiff from the north side river. I now camp sneakily near glimmering farm home lights and dancing river boats from across the way. Acoustic humming, fine whistling and wine sipping, I wonder... Am I in A cow pasture? Better to sleep now than later.

St. Nicholas is in smelling distance, and I'm on a stomping bull's turf. I crawl through the page wire fence, dragging my paraphernalia in tow; the red-eyed black bull stands pawing the sod twenty yards away on the bank top. Safe and packed, I cross the Timothy to the highway gravel. Yesterday was grand for the sweet taste of vineyard flow. Costly on mileage.

Friendly waves and warm handshake invite me to feast in an over-ripe garden, filling the body to slumber on. I cross A high steel span bridge entering the city on Fortress Hill, "Bonne chance," and every smile that goes with friendly gestures. The streetlights mark yellow rows before the arch entrance to the old cobble street as I hear the vibrant songs of this culture's people. No one listens in the dark stream murmur. I cross through rows of evening trembling elms, run A sweated hand along the mounted monumental ball cannon, and walk on stubby well-cut grass to the center of the Plains of Abraham. I drop my home to sleep among pigeon-stained and plastered war-gazing figures. No sooner bedded for sweet slumber when A patrolman's' flashlight shines blinding into my face. I explain and show papers of recognition. Being courteous to the Centennial Walker, I'm allowed to rest for this one night on the battle memorial field. "Au revoir".

Hopping mechanically, the robin dew-worm-searcher flies in solitude upon Abraham's Plains. I peek out into the one hand bright sunrise morning, thinking of the twenty extra miles I have walked. I'm crying to bathe my pus-running body.

The St. Joan of Arc statue is in the garden of rowed flower beds, and many people ride in the horse-drawn two-seat buckboard on Old City cobblestone streets. I descend from Quebec City, chattering among Levis's riverboat crossers. To U, Frontenac and the gleaming city old, I salute with milk and bread. I bid farewell, cherrio citadel.

Towards Montmagny, under the finest of sunny days, the high riverbank touches A seaward-smelling scenery with the widening river. It's a lurching climb among large and small willow on A shale clay hundred-foot bank, and I need bathing. Loud highway noise disturbs the silence of the mind, and loneliness is alone, I mean very alone, among private fenced property and many questioning motorists. I stand now in water and land.

Dripping from the falling heaven moisture, my pack is leaned on cement steps. I walk into the granite stone church among sober statues; a repentant traveler with mixed emotions. I enter the last pew, and although I'm much too early for service, I meditate with courageous prayer. The quietness lies deep within the walls of the sanctuary. Why does every stale white face, clean cut with bonnet pink, glare at me in this last pew? I feel itchy and uncomfortable, more than the poison ivy, and I exit before service on Sunday, August twenty-seven rains.

St. Roche Des Aulnets has wood carvings placed on display in shop windows. The sad humpback, oiled-skin fisherman twinkles under his sou'wester and beams at eye level at the dripping passerby in such cool changes of weather. The habitant is learning in thought on his three-prong pitchfork, and A milkmaid stands with two buckets. Ohh, for most carvers, the village turns commercial, but I could not jingle more than three dollars and thirteen cents for A fifty-dollar sculptured carving. The brown, long-stringy, seaweed-smelling Maritime'ish bedding is made among large boulder rocks. Nailing new steel clickers with A stone, I tighten the Dutch strap and climb up the granite bank to greet the two-hands rising sun.

From the highway entrance into Riviere du Loup, I view the ship loading below at the pulp and peat moss cargo dock. Chain gang loading workers, with oily sweat brown backs, is A continual ant-working circle. I lonely turn from the river and soberly smile among painted faces and laughing comments as the majority of villagers gape. I round slowly over the hill, and wave A kiss goodbye to the wonderful scenic St Lawrence River. There's A brick wall warehouse that has written in large white letters, "Welcome To Sin City Canada", and here's to U old rattling town. Thinking for A moment about the jingling that I reach to count, only twenty-seven cents, and that is for valid grub till reaching seventy-six miles, the City of Edmundston. Bleak peat moss fields that I pass, which workers have cut into blocks, is piled like step pyramids to dry the organic fuel. I find bushes of ripe blueberries and eat the fat of the land.

Beyond St. Honore, on the second fasting day, the cool mist Atlantic showers blow over the well-greened summer scenery. I increase to two vitamin tablets at mid-day, double the water supply for the stomach, and force twenty-five more miles. The cool rainwater drips from my long peak cap into the feverish red eyes that long for A solid meal and a warm, dry bed. The ivy scabs I do not feel, and I know they are getting better. Ohh, Madonna of Nature, how good "art thou"! A green apple tree, stomach filling, sour but thankful.

Friday, September the first; I bundle up my wet tent and staggeringly strap the house-pack on sagging shoulders, feeling like the corpse of somebody else. A day, yes, A day to remember. A fifth child, oh poverty, that hurts the meek. Here standing in rags, bare feet,

146

holding A small paper cup of French fries to sell to fly past motorists, is A golden straw-haired ten years old girl. A reality of need. In A low bush yard stands A small tar paper shack with windows card boarded, lives her family with A handful of younger brothers and sisters. I draw the last ten coppers. Gently she smiles, "merci". The discouragement and hunger, the steps, all is forgotten. Explained by A garage owner that many families are like this; there is little work, some in pulp; "U are now in the Maritimes." I sew "La Belle Province" crest of Quebec. How warm were your friendly morning smiles and family suppers!

As the Madawaska flows, I enter the Edmundston Post Office in New Brunswick and reach for the mail. I receive a letter from home and a brown envelope cheque. I have one hundred and ten dollars from the government. God, this means food, and I run out bashing the guitar neck pack on the glass "entrée" door.

It was A child with A meek smile
Counting the years are long, and clothes were worn
A rose she gave for my mind did crave.

Chapter 14

LOVE FABULATION....

There is some grayness in the sick-smelling weather, and heaven's clouds roll rumbly from the Atlantic Northeast. I stash my ten bill travelers' cheques on the center page of the black book log. Buckling down, the Dutch strap tightens two holes tighter; there is weight loss, for I can't B heavier than one thirty. Trampling across the Madawaska River on A cement passage, I look deeply among the blue-rich swirl foamed by A sudsy waste solution. It drains from A trough run-off from the bank pulp mill.

Late mid-day rest, I'm trying A compulsory regular meal before losing out and fading away into the dust. The fall-like storm winds creep upon and tears with the cold North Atlantic rains, splashing the village of Riviere Verte. I'm seated among the spruce green hills and lazy river below, one mile West. My tea fire sputters, turning black as I lean back, resting against this thick-branched white spruce. The last bite of bread soaked in the canned stew gravy, I watch restfully while sipping the green tea. Goshawk gliding, his peeling eyes for his fauna "coup de grace" evening meal, is a graceful bird in flight. Evening gray mist flows upon A tinted-coloured hue, and sweat runs off a black peak band into two burning eyes. The freight cries a low bellow, winding and rattling on ocean rail, heading Southeast on the riverbank.

148

The night started with the expulsion of A thousand sand drumming flies, screaming their existence around my little castle domain. Finally, the cool rain, noise like a Gatling gun, drowns them to everlasting slumber. I'm beyond Siegas, St Leonard and Belle Fleur, in A bank wooded area three miles from Grand Falls. All spruce needles hang with tingle crystal adroitness like Christmas decorations. I'm wet to the bone and chilled. Wonder when will the snow blow? The year sure looks ominous.

The flying transport tires hiss and whistles while carrying the load down Trans Canada Highway blacktop to the industrial machine. "My! This road is high!" I could reach out over the Grand Falls, N.B. house roof. A heavy falling dew from North-west cools my weary bones on A traffic busy Labour Day fourth Monday morning. They speed and rush home for morning work after A tiring weekend. I wonder... Is that "the kind of behavior that brings out insults? U screwball ugly." I'm yelled at and spat upon, and I jump into the ditch from the highway shoulder chase; that nut tried to run me down. Most local hoods hit the road for the weekend sun rest, probably their last before the North flake blow.

"Hello, young fellow, shake the hand of A good Irishman."

"Your Irish, Sir?"

"Yes indeed, pure blood."

"Oh, when did U arrive in Canada?"

"Been here all my life, but Dad comes from the Republic Cork."

"Then that makes U Irish? I see."

"Yes, but I'm no foreigner, I hate them greasy loafers. Come in young fellow and have tea with I, here at the Café."

"What A swell name, Bath." A fine name for my water-loving body, and the sweat-scummy sleeping sack is almost A perishable chamber. Upper Kent, above the Beachwood Dam, flows housing run-off sewer that slimes up my soaped-upon body. I'm slime dirtier than the sour sweat."

Tiny baby ducks dance merrily past the Florenceville town on the old John riverbank. The time flies with the aging year, and yellow loose leaves float in A gliding saucer form to rest and stick on the dew-licked tent. Now the evenings have cooled, and flies are scarcer and scattering, crawling into cracks of tree stumps and cedar pole fences. The sundown early with my hand-time changing in this third dwindling season, and I'm only in the beginning of this fall period.

Northeast blue and white rolling fall clouds with gleam fading peek-a-boo sun paints rays of color in shades of green surrounding round river bank hills. Each day the green steeped tea warms my inside; what appreciation I have for the slight change of weather.

The slime-run river is disregarded and hidden in this blue God-touched country. Many wild ducks graze triumphantly among the diced vegetable and scum scraps of sewage that frames the Saint John,

N.B. sluice. This morning I clicked the board walkway across the 1285 feet, the longest covered bridge of the globe; Hartland, N.B. On the river's west bank and gazing while seated, I eat two oranges and drink four raw eggs; A breakfast tribute to the genre landscape.

Woodstock, U look aged from this upper hotel window, and the leaves are gathering on drainage grates along street curbs. I take the third and final bath, which has to do for another perspiring week unless I find A clear stream. The day has an Indian summer wine dip, and sol warms against the back chill North-west dry, cool blow. I'm winding slowly with long strides uphill, around curves to a valley low on new highway construction, where the river dam ahead floods sixty miles upstream. All river valley farm homes are either being destroyed or hauled uphill from rising water; fertile gardens are drowned, joining the muddy river bottom.

This cabin is fields across under birch and spruce grove, and the dusk evening owl hoots, answering my anxious search. The screen pops loose, the window slides, and I crawl in, cooking up my remaining rations and sack out on a single bare spring bunk. The hair-scaled, long-tailed scum of a rat wakes me as his beady red eyes looks upon Hank's lonely body. This chaos ends abruptly when a five-pound boot is tossed. I light a candle and wait out the darkness.

Under the Pokiok constructed bridge on my winding dust-choking road, I pry the steps forward through Prince William and Kings Clear, watching the cement-lifting cranes pour into forms of the newly built Mactaquac Dam.

On Saturday, abusive insults from youth passer-by follow with my strides in their double whip-aerial punk-heap car. The streamline insults level to nerve my weary walk. Passing swanky homes, I curve under weeping willows and maple-shadowed trees on the East riverbank entry to New Brunswick capital, Fredericton.

All empty and alone, the food does not settle my growling stomach. A city center café with people strangely looking my appearance structure over, I keenly feel the stares. I contemplate upon A black stone, red-eyed jewel Buddha seated in meditation on board window sill. "Slipper-sliding" Sam, the Chinaman keeps U polished slick. Dusk darkness falls upon the hot streets of the city. Many groups of fun-loving students have brotherly trials to enter their fraternity clan. The laughs echo loud among the elm-shaded streets. "North to Alaska, ha ha." Pushing the pack high with anger, I look for the street number; Noel, A sweet friend.

September eleventh; At high noon Monday, I look at the eyes of the boss owners and green-suited businessman who gather for A Kiwanis club dinner. Hank, the guest, is nervous. I feel the refusal and disbelief from the careless questions. My financing is explained, and I am given A job on construction ten miles back, North-west below the Mactaquac Dam.

"Noel, your beginning of A new week is similar to A breaking delay of my constant walk."

"But Henri, I remain here for A year in college surrounded by green sickly walls of this apartment, and U only for one week."

"Oh, Noel, that is how you've been feeling."

She looks "stretchingly" posed from the second-floor window upon the back alley, where kids play their rock war games. She is sweet, tiny and "Frenchify".

"U will visit while working the week at the upper dam?"

"Yes, I have to find A camp location before dark; I will probably return A few evenings from today."

Peering at the dew fog cloud morning on John riverbank, I tie the high part tent on A hanging wild cherry branch, then have A sandwich for breakfast on top of two raw eggs. Taking A short walk towards squeaking machinery through the rising fog, the second work job day begins with the grasping of the shovel handle. The large cubic cement water storage vats will hold millions of tiny salmon and larger vats for the spawning mature salmon. "How will they survive the swim through the slime?"

About midnight the third day, while resting, A crawling animal scratches my face, and with waking fright, I jump to the low back end of the tent. My hand reaches timidly to grasp the small flashlight. Yellow glare frightens the coon, and it scuffles to re-enter its outside riverbank world, but the tent flap holds low like A lid trap door. The raccoon sits perched at the zippered door, ready to spring for my throat. Finally gathering the courage for the onset, and with A large boot in hand, I clobber the innocent striped creature. I crawl from my bag and tent, holding my victim by his pretty tail. Then, an idea in mind; I chisel with my hacker knife the trophy tail then toss the remains below the bank on a sandy river beach. I may have begun A new era of species, A bob-coon. Holding high the tail, I complete A thorough search at daybreak along the riverbank for the corpse, but either it's been cannibalized or has regained its consciousness. I have lost this struck-down creature.

The days of A moulded year are perturbed in dust cloud memories. I wonder at the arrow-piercing message that could have reached but has not. Now, I am haunted by winter's reminder of snow and sleeping out. "Or is it my stubborn determination that burns the beacon light?"

The St. John River has smothered two more victims in its swirling blue void. Last night A machine engineer and his helper, while working their clam crane along the river shoal, capsized into the dugout eddy. The murmuring echoes of A moaning cow across the river reminds me of the whispering thought of A short life cycle before all enters the soil dust of maggots.

A friendly fist-full of gathered friends frolic in their boisterous singing. It is Sunday morning before I realize that my guitar string fingers are blistered and swollen. I slept under the corner table on A hard floor bedding, curled up in the bag.

"U lazy bums, when does the rise of early crow come for you? I went to church already, and it's late noon."

"Noel, never mind the church growling."

Each room corner is evacuated, and friends gather for A mid-day spaghetti dish, shoulder to elbow, around A miniature table.

I shuffle on down to the street corner block church, and inside by the coloured painted features, the quietness surrounds me in prayer and song. The church has empty stillness, and only the alter candle flickers. I write two words on my Journal Page.

"Winter coming."

I am now on the return to my riverbank camp, bidding farewell to my cheery friends, A great bunch from the Northern N.B. shore and A sweet bye-kiss from Noel; I return to work, bored to tears and worrying of winter coming soon.

I'm continuing the walk; it's early mid-day sun on this leaf withered painted month. Jim hands me my cheque.

"All the best, Hank."

"Thanks, this ninety-six dollars of food money will carry the journey to its distant end."

From the riverbank hatchery, A gray dusty road traverses windward in tailgate dust to the busy penetrating black ribbon highway. I whistle to the birds of a gathering flock; such happiness is the feeling on my voyage while the sash band and knife dangles on right hip. The autumn vegetation dies on this eve of grayness. I blow kisses upstream on the lazy John River from Princes Margaret Bridge.

There's A clumsy form that scales the page wire fence as I retreat into the dusk dew cedars to pitch camp.

The green of love shy
With games can make U cry
Butter, sweet lips and candy apple pie.

Walker Arrives On PEI

Hank Gallant of Nail Pond, Centennial marathon walker who travelled on foot from Beacon Hill BC, arrived in Borden last night. He spent the night in the port town where he took a room and took a refreshing bath. Once a week he spends the night in a hotel or motel and the remainder of the week he camps out.

Carrying a 50-pound pack on his back, Mr. Gallant left Beacon Hill near Victoria, British Columbia at 9 a.m. on February 6 with his destination being St. John's, Newfoundland. The cross-country walk is Mr. Gallant's personal centennial project and he refuses to take any lifts from motorists.

Mr. Gallant left Borden early this morning and expects to reach Charlottetown around noon on Friday where he will visit Confederation Centre. He will then walk to Wood Islands and travel by car ferry to Nova Scotia on his journey to Newfoundland.

To date Mr. Gallant says that he has lost a total of 27 1/2 pounds since he first began his Canada-wide walk.

Mr. Gallant, who expects to write a book on his cross-Canada jaunt, was born in Nail Pond, PEI and left there five years ago. He is the son of Mr. and Mrs. Alyre Gallant of Nail Pond. He also has a sister, Mrs. Frank Doucette, residing in Nail Pond. These members of his family will meet him in Charlottetown as he does not plan to come west until he has completed his journey.

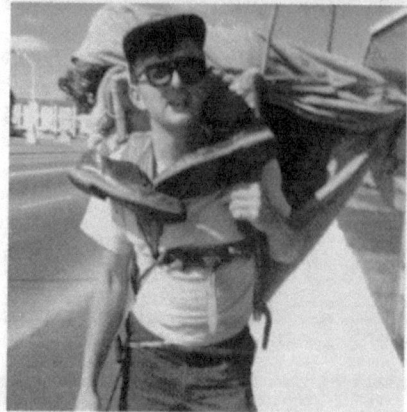

Chapter 15

BREATHES THERE A MAN....

The turbulent ocean mist from across the stunned swamp spruce is refreshing; as seated, I play Gibson in happy fulfilment of my dream with reality. The coil hay in a five-acre backfield, with partly sun-dried daffodil, nests the mattress of tranquility. There yonder, in a "swaley" swamp, the gathered black-breasted flock shriek their hungry search for remaining wild chokecherries. Will the birds remain to sing and play? Aah! But it is fall, and determination drives me on as I rise to sing my song on the eastward left gravel shoulder.

Their loyalist flag of crimson rag waves staunch ward from the Gulf Stream breeze. The Motts were the ones who had cheered for the Queen and felt that the red crimson leaf should B left on the trees. I enter for food into the store to the gling-glong bell.

"What can I do for U, Sir?"

She looks half-frightened and wants to get rid of me in A hurry.

"Two apples, one orange, four eggs, cheese, bully beef and bread."

"Is that all today, Sir?"

I chuckle.

"Yes, today."

Her colour tints to rust-rose when asked. "Why is the Legion and most tourist homes in this location flying the British flag high and not our new distinguished Canuck Flag?"

"We fought under that flag, mind U I didn't, but neighbours about did, and for my likings, the new rag, as I see it, looks too much like the Canada Meat Packers flag," she replied.

Jemseg and Grand Lake; bathing in cold water with chills, I towel the sweat salt pores clean. Forgetting to observe for the campsite, I pay too much attention to towns and welcoming signs, like Mill Cove, Water Borough and Young's Cove, when suddenly someone aims to scare merely yards behind the Coles Island sign, partly hidden at late dusk. I had dismantled minutes before in A vacant willow shrub when A rifle-packing Coles man blares his aimed warning.

"Hey U, do U hear? Get clear of this land, U have ten seconds to move, or I'll shoot U right between the dials."

In a flash, I toss-drag the pack out to the highway, eyeing the rifleman as he moves downfield in retreat watch.

Turning over on my stomach, the daybreak September peak is fashioned with nose entering autumn dew morning while hauling on my hiking clobbers. A "Coureur de Bois" starvation diet is an imaginable reality, but great lettuce with potato salad and eggs is a super feast. I close my eyes without thought and smell the heavenly air that flows among the rolling harmonious hills. I realize with apprehension on the theme of this venture. The wild notion has caused A small stir within and around my person. With a different abstract, the long blacksnake road is A challenge. The Coureur de Bois, A small copy in mind to follow those large footsteps succession. A cry of wild free life in his birthright Canada, the "Coureur" trapper escaped from the Law Council and Priests, the beginning of A new society. Alexander Ross described one individual trader as A liberated son of the wilderness who hunts in freedom while trading in Indian country and having qualities of A brave venture. "Huzza! Huzza! Pour le pays sauvage."

South-east of Long Creek among the birch top hills of many rolling contours, I crawl from under A nylon shelter, stretching A mile-yard to greet the brisk white frost morning. Death is the smell of floating leaves, like fallen soldiers on mud blood covered forest gray. There beyond the verge of fog stands A crow viewing on A spruce, hand measured in heavens blue on 2100 feet hill crest. Overnight the frost falls now the sun breaks through a rising cloud. My world enters A skip hop jubilant paradise, and nature marks its first spectrum disguise. The high sun glows on the engraved twenty-second of September.

With hand gestures, while the sun slowly sets South-west, I cool burning feet in one of many hill-flowing streams. I carefully check and pick some loose callous skin around my heels along the instep. Changing boots and socks, I enter with bold, happy steps into Sussex Valley green. A fine view with sun on left shoulder, I descend from west highway tone hill. Sol sits one hand high without any success to warm the offense from ignorant minds. Queried insults along the tunnel-elm streets are like A frightened nightmare.

"Would they kill for what I do? Are their minds filled with jealousy?"

"U damn fool, shorts in the fall, U weirdo."

I hide in A four-dollar room to cry my weary mind; does it get worst further East? At time it has punctured, but my question hits with a forceful blow: "Is it worth the effort?"

I accelerate from my bough-bedding nest in A morning of haste, and skilled for survival, I carefully find dry birch bark and dead spruce branches for A quick spirit fire. McQuack hums from A hanging green branch over the fire, and buttered steakettes sizzle inside its foil wrapping on the red coals. A light splatter of rain falls on dried cadmium leaves. Layers of plummeting high branches shape the pinnacle spruce. In the shelter, I exercise the formation of ideas. I gaze on bush wild forest and the few remaining touches that man has not destroyed. Two miles or less from village Penobsquis where black spruce tend high, we converse in friendly chat an Indian Micmac and I.

"Where U come from, Hank? Have U met many Indians?"

"Yes, in Northern B.C."

"They find work easy in B.C., eh?"

"Well, I believe so."

"U believe, but that's not here in New Brunswick, no work, no hunting I'm like A Jacob, I stay at home and plant A garden for food."

161

I pass A chicken farm up on the hill left, which looks like A snow-white field of feathers. Behind this roasting imagination sits two old dry croaking crows hoping for dinner of A weak chicken. Old Sol's bright warmth on my country falls abruptly, obscured in the West bank cloud. In forms of flight, the two ravens' "nock-ock" a deep throat sound, and "stuntly" as an acrobat in flight, they rise over rolling hills like painted pictures. Playing ravens are like barometers, they tell of A wet day tomorrow. The part that fails my mind when trying to subside the feeling of loneliness is that one cannot take tomorrow's dreary wet day as A persistent worry but accept each dawn. Once your inner soul determines its achieved goal to accomplish, your body will follow, and U in your harness will B like an obedient nag.

Night falls crow-black on this New Brunswick brook bank. How strong the twinkling North Star penetrates the rising clouds, then in moments, obscured like gathering birds, they all vanish in the South wind. Cloudy mist fog creeps gray before daybreak, surrounding the solemn tree trunks. Snapping flames burn to red glowing coals, and a fork branch holds my steakettes. Three eggs drank, bread and steak, warm and fed. I join the road where the brook slides under the highway in a swampy swale.

Hillside winds and rain pound the black spruce and highway from Petitcodiac to Moncton on this Sunday soaked with rain. Numb feet feel the water between toes, and I have walked twenty-nine miles today. Moncton entry road, the contrast of green sloped washed fresh fields to mud gray carved slough on the valley floor is caused by

Fundy's high rising tides. All these natural views are screened through sweat-burning eyes. Now, all my will is geared toward the city center and A cheap dry room.

Stiff, tired and swollen feet with blood-clotted callouses, I wake being strangled by A white sheet rolled about my neck; it's all A rotten dream.

Down through the city on C.N. tracks, I wave at gapes in wonder till I reach Church Street. Like batman, the reporter springs from his parked car, a brown tight fitted suit, hair speared on the sides of his drab black hat, and A vigour boldness in his grasping approach. He positions himself in many angles, A curb lay down and bridge aerial view.

Splashing muddy shoulder on Road no 2 towards Shediac, I smell the fresh sweet spray from Northumberland waters and the sixty miles that separate me from home; it's a cry of A happy longing.

The pastry delivery chap tells me of the morning reporter looking on the Trans-Canada for A Walker. It's moose-hunt opening day; he takes pictures of the earliest big trophy kills at nine A.M., and in a rush, the reporter forgot his film. I chuckle when leaving the Smith's Corner Café. The outlook has completely changed as high cool winds roll in waves from the North-west, and seagulls glide in search of sandy beach. Acadian North Shore French adopts English words that spices the accent.

East of Pointe du Chene, sheltered behind A grove of shrub-stunned evergreens on a sand dune shore, I view longingly over briny back waves to the twinkling window lights from Island rocking in the Gulf. The driftwood fire snaps warmly as sand dunes gain from the lonely wind void. Smelling dry flaked cod or maybe "Couleur de rouge", boiled lobster, I dream on nights ocean roar.

September twenty-sixth: Beautiful clear cold sting finger morning, I carry my pack down the road through Cap Pele and Shemogue after Sol has failed his mid-day warmth on autumn fresh cold wind. To the left on gravel dust Cape Bruin road, evening finds me searching the abandoned house by the hilltop overlooking white cap bay. The spine-chilling bats glide freely through the open hole of a second-story window. I hide with gnawing mice on the corner floor; "forest ghosts are much softer than house ghosts."

Across the mouth cliff bay to the open sea, the shifting wind draws salt morning tears while gaping from this open hole peak. U are sure alone; good-bye, gray mouse, so cute. In A subterranean dream-smile while kicking pebbles on a sandy road, a vicious dog suddenly lurches into my mid-day path. From behind A turkey coup ranch, snarling and teeth frothing. A challenging German shepherd leaps for my throat. The flashing blade draws out, and I roll with the charge. White teeth with hair raised and snarling at bay, I'm on one knee, and the knife is ready. "Hey, fella, he won't bite. Come on, boy, come home. He never seen such an odd thing." Heart pounding, brain contact with cold sweat drops, I stand cursing the mad dog. Within the scared numb silence, I tremble with each stumbling step.

Late afternoon sun brightens warmly, and I lurk in shocked readiness at every dog bark. Here's to U the last steps on N.B. soil, and up the gangplank and to Abegweit Ferry deck. Many words I could describe for the toast of another victory. While crossing the Northumberland Strait, I sew the New Brunswick crest on a black ball cap. Watching the sunset's ball over the blue water strait, I tinkle inside with happiness of reaching home Island.

Love Of Country

Breathes there the man, with soul so dead,

Who never to himself hath said.

This is my own, my native land!

"Sir Walter Scott."

Isn't it beautiful in its own special way, the non-leisure moments of my world in my time, and umpteen interval chats like most Maritimers "nice and easy." It's late evening dusk after A forty-five-minutes crossing from Tormentine to Borden. Rising to the procedure of ferry disembarking, I struggle with triangle pack magnitude around car fenders and aerials. The feeling of home longing has never before been so strong. I skip hop the gangplank as A lump catches my throat in breath. Sunrays, in Westward disappearance, are kissing the twilight of A perfect day to this blood-red soil. Lateness causes no worry; I splash in cool salt water and sponge the pores with nature's taste. It chills me, and I hurry in hump-back stride through Borden village. How refreshing was that Harbour dip. It's all so real, lying here under a short green bush with a sleeping bag and tent while a canvas floor separates me from red sweet soil of home.

I rush about in A morning of pure fall weather, happy to B on P.E.I. and yet, it's not "really" home. I stand, knee pressing against the Albany turn-about rail. Seventy-five longing miles to the colorful tinted rusty sand mound shores, where I raced wild Pete in a flappy buckboard. What A horse! Kicked the dashboard to hell. Unique names of Sea Cow Pond, Skinners Pond and Nail Pond, "that's for sure", A maritime saying.

From this highway height above Tryon settlement in September sun, there aloft, across "vert" emerald swales and fields, is a bay rescue chopper. It traverses in solemn search for another sign of life, floating among the green-blue ocean billow waves. Further East, among the easy-rolled green hills that blends with matching red soil, the season's Spud Island harvest has begun. Trucks heaped with flowery sweet potatoes rattle to the warehouse bins. Combine harvesters dig and swallow the fertile rows to the chains where stock and rocks are removed by busy hands, then to the waiting truck box. The white-skinned spuds roll on a tender cushion soft, A circle of continuance from seed to growth, then harvest.

I pass the sweet blind stares of Crapaud villagers in windows, giggling and finger-pointing, being very shy in their curious ways. I dust the red gravel shoulder in the evening twilight after A generous Blue Goose-Café supper and A chat with the world-at-ease proprietor. Hours pass in damp dew blight smell, turning green drying grass and all sweet summer verdure to death as autumn rolls.

I finally arrive at Strathcona Park, an evergreen hillside. I pass through the gate and follow a black winding road over A valley bridge of a gurgling brook, where in the far corner, A rain shelter is picked for my camp bedding. Rolling over in rays of A perfect sunrise morning, I, as in times before, sing and play old Gibson to the green-on-red rolling farmland. After A two-bit shower, I enjoy one-half quart of milk, four eggs, sweet bread and honey, and as A topper, a hunk of cheese. Within A mind disturbed by loneliness, I have changed my attitude. I'm now happily striding for Charlottetown City, where friends and family I hope will come. Passing the Kingston Legion, where the Union Jack flies high, there is A reserved feeling as I glance; I don't want to cut the flag down.

Just A singing up Elm Avenue in the moist before the rain, I cross King St., where the bronze war soldiers with prepared bayonets for a battle charge through the questioned rains of yesterday. The contour statuary "Confederation Centre" is a concrete block mold and plain like its finest virgin soil, standing like a labyrinth; it's a small memory for the present of the past when Canada was formed. Echoing in happiness through crowds of Saturday shoppers, I receive one letter at Post Office and then find A thirty-two-bit room on Kent Street.

In the silence of A drip tap basin and A smoked painted white impregnable room, the impact of city hustle tickles in blood veins. The finger snap-knock and the room door swings open. The walls are filled with happy faces; all my friends of two years I have not seen. Yes, some descendants of the green; count them many who came across in dory boats during the Potato Famine, "Hey man, how in hell are U?" All standing in a circle, gaping and talking. Friend Ed with his smiling wife, sings my favorites, the "Patriot Game" and "Rambling Boy."

"Let's have A jam session."

"That's A welcome."

"Hank, tear open the mouth harp."

The older folks join. Like the fog that rolls in, the toe-tapping music fades away in my four-by-four room. Then, all is gone; they have all went West to the other end of this Island; they may return with more friends and family.

Without an ounce of sleep in the early morning mist of splattering rain, with the silent step of light shoes, the clobber heavy hike boots are slung over my shoulder. I round the street corner and pass A music shop in the silence of this damp sleepy morning.

"It'll B noon before they're ready."

"Fine, give them the works, new nylon soles, heels and horse-shoe clickers."

September thirtieth: On the street from the cobbler shop like the fresh beginning of this day, wide-eyed in A happy chuckle, I whistle my echoed way through the morning-work staring crowd. "I knew an old lady who lived in A shoe, yeh ho for the shoe." My knowing that family and friends will B here, I march these Confederation step in needle nerve wait.

Loaded with happiness and home jar food of the best, my parents, grandma, brother, sister, and her husband and son, with all the crowd that was here last night, have returned.

"Let's go to your room, Hank."

"Immediately."

"Got A feed of the red cooked lobsters," explained Fred.

To the statement, I only "ummm" in reply, then devoured half A dozen and three "red fellas" without raising A twinkle from the paper box that holds these beauties.

"The manager is getting very upset with stair traffic and all the music noise; would U hold it lower, or U may all leave."

"Aouh, she's an angry lady."

Ed rebuts in limey brogue.

Later we are standing on Kent in early darkness chill, expressing farewells in good journey handshakes. Mothers' cheeks are wet, worrying about where Hank will sleep tonight because the Hotel manager ordered us out. One thousand more miles with songs in the night, as mist drips among pillars on steps of the old Confederation Chamber, Ed, his wife, and I play till our fingers get cold then numb in this last of September night. City kids walk by us on the way to the corner box Presley Show. Some sit to listen till our strings break twang, then home so long friends. I beg the clerk to let me in my paid room. "Then U better be quiet."

All packed and ready for tomorrow's highway, it has been so great to reach home soil and friends. I sprawl out on A bed with cloud-reprieved dreams.

To reach
To find
To B happy.

CROSS CANADA HIKER WITH 3,800 MILES BEHIND HIM, PUSHES ONWARD

Cross- Canada marathon walker Hank Gallant takes a breather beside the Trans-Canada Highway, near New Glasgow, Tuesday as the 24-year-old British Columbia construction worker continues his historic walk across the nation. His arrival in Nova Scotia marked his 239th day since leaving Victoria, B.C., 3,800 miles ago. He plans to complete the trip in mid-November. (Townsend photo)

Chapter 16

THE OX LAND KILT....

The sun rises among bird-nested elms. I hear the early seven "glong" of down street corner church, and all is lonely and still within this rough plastered room while eating a sandwich breakfast. It's a bruising struggle downstairs with the pack through the hallway. Outside among family strode sidewalks, I toss pack high on right shoulder, slip left arm through shoulder straps and buckle the Dutch belt.

I echo-whistle among the gray smoke redbrick houses on a sunny sleepy Sunday morning. Crossing with clubbing steps over Hillsborough River Bridge on October first, the breeze blows moist fresh Northumberland Strait. There's A gaiety for spring walking with the thought of early fall snow, then journeys end. Island neighbours, who visit Sunday relations, stop to chat with mocking jargon. "Whatcha doing?" She in the back says, "my, what a load, got the stove and sink?" I ignore them, turning with eyes to view A honking gander and his wild Canadian formation flock. Cursing, the occupants squeal on gravel sprayed highway from the opposite shoulder; then head towards Charlottetown. My blood runs boiling; for this is not a good welcome.

Old sol hides softly in A submerged island of trees along the Lord Selkirk Park. I'm satisfied with twenty-four miles, and heading into the two-bit shower house, I stand in complete loneliness afresh. The red shale bank of the bay, with A hundred bobbing-honking wild geese, reminds me that I should go south instead of east. This adopted oil cast stove, when stocked, hums up on a pipe draft with a block of birch and balsam-gummed white spruce, warming comfortably this under rain shelter. Wrapping a sleeping bag with a tent on top of a hard table, I lie while A dancing star-quilt of midnight lightens those hundred thoughts. The wild gander calls on a chill autumn night; it may rain. "Sleepy, sleepy, good-night."

Rise and shine U silly cause, hidden in the cozy warm bedroll. Among the stand-bars foamy white cap bay, rising from the fresh cool North-west flow of wind, I hear loud honks of lifting wild geese who graze in the field of farmers in the high light sun. I chomp on breakfast's last remaining meat pie crumbs, then belt the "swaller" of water, washing the last taste to a growling stomach. Fall grays have lightened the youth of growth, yet the green grass of many fields blends its tickle-tact with "couleur rouge" on fresh fall-plowed fields. Seagulls pick, gather bugs and worms; crows complain with anger from the tinge-veiled grove. I look in silence from the curb-hill road where the Island walk ends. This I give thanks for steps made on native land, visited by dear friends and relations of old. Slowly on schedule time of four hands falling sun, I push forward while suck licking the marrow berry jam inside the roll tart crust. I sing my mind with heartfelt songs as passengers sit in silent stares on Wood Island Caribou Ferry. The diesel-propelled ship glides across God's evening on aurora blue sparkling strait; the hued garden that sits rocking in the gulf.

"U sing deep thoughts, do U feel like that?"

"Especially this evening, while sewing the P.E.I. crest on my cap."

"But what about yourself? You look lonely."

Beyond Pictou on New Glasgow, Nova Scotia shortcut, I pitch a tent high on a meadow ridge under A tall-sole elm. My mind wanders to those golden curls that left in the back seat of an American Caddy. One foot after another, I hold them in sizzling relief; they burn, so cooked. Water is brook fresh cool held in the small soak pan. Oh, what A sensation to rub the cold, moist over burnt tissues, cleaning the sweaty pores. I sack where I smell the soil on my face, having dreams under bare ghost elm.

New Glasgow street, where English and black sparrows shriek and churp, are among the rows of park benches along a gravel pathway. Smells blend with my elevated hunger at mid-day sun, while autumn North-west blows from salt chuck bay. Entering A fish joint, I'm served by A cute blonde "upsy nosey" waitress and order the famed fish and chips with tea dinner.

I re-enter onto Highway 2, and inside A grocery store, I buy four eggs, two oranges, sweet bread, burger meat and onion. On steps changing boots and socks, I place food in a small carrying bag along with China tea from town café. I'm A good gentleman at peace with life. Coming to my approach is A scattered group of bus-riding school kids who choke in dust smoke cloud when their yellow carrying vehicle moves away in gear-shift grind.

"Hey, he's the guy who's walking!"

"No kidding, must B crazy."

"U wouldn't walk to school U big mouth."

"Now Alice, U just like thrills."

It's funny, sitting here contemplating on the brief sunset evening, and they gather around arguing over my form and idea.

"Now, honestly, fella, U can't sit there looking smart and tell us that U have walked from B.C. here without taking A ride. Just sneak riding A few miles?"

"Defeat my challenge, the walk and dream idea?"

"Hell, if it was me, I'd sneak A ride in the back of an old truck."

"Cherrio, good evening."

"Darn, your crazy; anyway, good luck."

Antigonish thirty miles, and only for the few irrelevant buzz fly-pass of autos, the forest where I sit would cry its silent tears. Tea warming fire glows four feet from the tent entrance, and McQuack forces A steady steam cloud from the funnel neck spout. The fall frost mist has risen to A moist Indian Summer October night. Biting bomber flies are frolicking in great clouds, with only A few too many on the battlefront. Playing A bit of how I feel blues, the notes echo through the distant swamp and scares me chilly. The fourth bowl of green tea always taste woody yellow; I rise to stretch under a nature branch roof to pick and break up dry wood in the fire glow light. Time anticipation haste for morning prompt tea and breakfast. Making up A pillow with a raincoat, I lie listening to thundering silence that rolls in my ears; makes me kiss to pray for what I feel and see. "Wild wilderness is the heaven where man is free, and all that lives to move."

Up at crow pee, two hours before the sun peeks the warm accelerated kiss, I putter the fire on breeze wave. Dump the remainder of strong tea on black smoldering coals and the road I hit hard, I mean tramp. Like other thirty-mile days, when reaching over twenty-five miles, it's A ton of weight and fried feet with worn heels and swollen ankles.

Antigonish Highland Game Park is only yards below the North Star on A dipper-hanging evening. I walk by the hardwood trees that span University lawns, where the New Scotia dream has touched their eager brains. Hiding from the sneers and laughs that bounce the pack high on the shoulder neck, I search out the Youth Hostel barn at A motel site. I shower and crawl clean to sleep under hip roof rafters. Sitting in wide-eyed darkness, the one and only window is attacked by A claw-winged bat. Knees drawn under chin in spine chill sweat, my teeth clatter as autumn light has reached here none too soon for my aspiration wish.

My echo steps are loud on the street sidewalk hours before the shop opening, as I wait for the cobbler by his door and share some sweet bread with the sparrows that linger among the streets for bits and pieces. Other birds of many-coloured feathers have flocked and sailed backwind to the Southland warmth. Bouncing little fluff birds are crumb-scrounging daily like beggars as the winter white deprives them of life vitality. The clouds fold in its heavy river pour. The leather boots are muddy, and white sweat film keeps moist-soft and conditioned for long wear; A great hiking boot compare with those five others. Lucky to have these extra light shoes, changing often on daily routine march, gives rest to my feet.

Farewells are tender even among newfound friends; I wave appreciation from the road, where hills of sparkly washed forest meet. So long Robinson Family, with hot roast beef, mash spuds and vegetables. He bats an eye on a grin form look, "nice to have U, Hank."

The dark fogged evening swirls around and covers the stranger, who is now an old friend. I disappear from view descending A sharp bend with long strides pushing me downhill. Autumn dusk clears with evening stars I may touch, feeling the dry, crisp cold that rolls behind the cloudbank eastward.

One foot of spruce branches are topped with thick remaining fluffed fir boughs. I wake with an early light peek as the smell of fresh balsam pillow blend with this after-rain fragrance. I drag out both the squirrel and the tea wood from under the tent shelter. Either I'm in his territory, or he wants to clear the odd shrub that is smoking him out of his tree. He bounces across a green branch path to A headwind sit, where now he combs face with the paw, the little noisy squirrel.

Tracadie, N.S. for A burger breakfast at four hands rising sun. People in warm kindness surrounds me closely on this familiar tip of Scots new land. East Antigonish School throws A welcome, and I'm found answering an auditorium full of questions.

Cars, how would I count them and people that stop, asking the same questions that try my soul for the past four thousand miles. Monastery by-pass: A monk, clicking camera from various angles, yells, "Hi!" Waving his arms, he pulls his frock from the door jam and spins on down the road, Brother Pedro.

Gray remaining light of evening, I'm gut-filled from A café of a hot chicken sandwich and A waitress cook that blends "Cuisine". I stand watching before crossing the Strait to the Island of Cape Breton. The windy cold screams among the power lines, and the pivot causeway bridge emits a gray battleship carefully through the lock. Darkness draws its quilt early on October cloudy night. Port Hawkesbury town-light dance merrily, and the dock beacon gives me the lonely creeps as I climb on Highway 4 by-pass. The page wire fence is downed with age; most cedar posts are broken at the soil level. In the outline of evening darkness, I stumble through tall highland dry grass and sheltered under this trio fir; I pitch a late camp.

The tent sags with inches of soggy first-fallen snow. From the wet quilt, I crawl, growling in chattering fright at this present shelter location. Directly below on the middle field path, a long black ribbon of mourning veiled people stumble silently in the slush to a freshly dug grave. Three black Cadillacs are parked close to the green mound pit. Once again, I slept in a boneyard. In thoughts of death, sorrow, white winter bite and hunger, I drop all things as is, charge down like a madman across the graveyard and over the rusty squeaking fence. Flopping with arms and legs, I pass the tranquil parked cars. One-quarter mile from the dramatic scene, drinking four coffees with burgers, I watch the snow fly from inside on a perched stool. I return to the grey-white graveyard hill, pack the soggy bedding, and head for the Highland Island. "May U rest in peace, whoever U are."

Speckle brush shrub, paint mixed with snow rain clouds and peeking sunshine on Highland marshes is A year to remember. Hospitality from James and Ferguson. I eat chocolate cake with icing, and my face is full of lobster sandwiches. Floated with tea and the valley winds have smothered the smell of A needed bath. I enter McPherson guest home and kingdom tub to snore in layered water. Nobody hits the "john" this evening; the bolt is drawn.

Sunday sunshine highway, near Louis Dale and St. Peters, is where six families on the twelve-mile road have invited me in for tea. Not to complicate bad feelings of A feather, I accept Reverend's invitation and stay neutral with cabbage rolls and Irish stew. Home tasty cooking.

Little Archie, A polite, shy young lad wearing a long peak cap, red shirt, blue jeans and sneakers, paddles his bike on the opposite shoulder, curious like many other village kids. He wheels two hundred yards ahead and studies me at a distance, but when he approaches to eye contact, he ignores my smile and retreats to backpack view. I break the ice.

"Hi, U been playing ball?"

"Oh, we had fun." "Whatcha doing?"

"Walking across Canada."

"Where's that?"

"To St John's Newfoundland."

"Gotta gun for hunting?"

"No, I try fishing for fun, times when I'm bored."

Like A piper of charm, the gathering of curiosity follows in shy astonishment across St Peters and lock Inlet Bridge. The many boats for pleasure are tied loosely on shifting tides after A Sunday afternoon of wave cutting on Bras d'Or Lake. A Dark bank of clouds cover the West falling sun, and today's warmth has melted yesterday's snow, forming A lake mist. Wonderful hospitality, "généreux". Yes! Try to imagine twelve of them families inviting me, this dusty road walker, for tea. It's A full course meal. I feel free to pitch a tent under A lake shore bush, empty alone with only tea, warm fire, guitar and much-needed sleep after twenty-four miles of walking.

Walking by Barra Head, Johnstown, and Cove of Soldiers and Irish, with boots squashing in the cold rain, I scream at these high hills that reflect the spitting clouds and bring just beauty to Bras d'Or Lake. Eating cold bully beef sandwiches on A new week madness, studying the bewildering signs of "Beware Mad Dog", "Private Property", "Prosecution for Trespassers and Keep Out" aggravate me. It's A U.S. mode to buy up these natural locations; barb wire surrounding summer castles which prevent U from dipping one little tow in A lake of your own. Frantic dilemma in the soaking rain, I crawl high over A ten-foot board fence to sleep on a sheltered veranda where the birds have gone South. Night creeps early on A damp open porch as I unroll and change into the last remaining dry clothes. Who but hops up boldly and struts two feet from my head, A Mr. Stink. There's no room for two up here. He turns in alert attention. I'm hungrier than U are, this is my bread, "skunk" out of here! Finally, the trespasser is relegated to the basement shelter. The rising wind swims fog with heavy rain around the floor-bedded soul. I wake in fright-worry that the four-legged black and white sneak smeller had returned, and the night pounds on in fury.

Where has...? But it's the tenth, and autumn North-east fog and drenched rain fills my boots. Fog covers my eyes when gray rolling hills funnel the windy current and leaves me splashing among thoughts. Thirty-three miles to Sydney and one-half milk chocolate washing A dime blueberry tart as I rest on Big Pond steps while changing calloused bleeding feet.

Eyes of a scavenger in a vigilant watch over the veiled storm-roaring East Bay is the gray-black, wing-tipped gull who picks the garbage clean on man's natural dump.

Sydney City, observed through burning eyes caused by sweat juice, is seeping from a long peak black cap. Waving to the nomad walker along the gravel shoulder entrance, the veterinarian invites me to his warm, dry, spare Hospital room.

"B comfortable, see U in the morning."

"Thanks."

Ragged wet clothes spread on the floor for hopeful drying, I'm warmly circled and wrapped in a bag sitting stiff with both feet swollen and bleeding lightly under hard split callous, soaking in a solution pan.

I crawl from A warm bed roll on A hard cot in A cement cold room cell, scaring me with claustrophobia. Clothes are soaked, and heading for the laundromat, I scare the Hospital Caretaker when he's bumped with the door.

"U frightened me, Boy."

"Oh, sorry."

"The Doctor did tell me of a traveler in the back room, but usually all doors are locked, even this back one. He occasionally gives room to different hobos."

"In his or your words, I'm A bum?"

"Well, aren't U?"

Outside in pick sharp October fall winds that sheet my wet clothes to an icy posture, I stride with backpack high; the jog may help cold-bite, as I rush to the laundromat. A fat blonde talk in desperate loneliness. Bouncing from pure chill, I scram to the washroom, change to dry clothes, and toss the remainder into the dryer. Hugging my guitar in happy warmth, I moan A blues song. My eyes are fixed on the pants. Oh, the crutch is chafed out from walking.

"No mail today Mr. Gallant."

"Are you sure Miss, not even one letter?"

"I'm sorry."

In Pretty Park, I shed the pack and stretch gapingly on A leaf-padded bench. One leg standing duck, he peeks with one eye open just A few yards on the bank; flocks of wild blacks and yet tamed are in this security. Small shelter houses are built on bank enclosure. The reflection on the lagoon from white stroked pair of swans heighten my world of blue. A crust of bread left to feed, I carry my emptiness with a pack to march the twelve miles to the ferry crossing.

Ten p.m. with a five-dollar ticket, I wonder where I can find a corner of quietness and snore the night loud. Outside on deck with a loud mixture of Harbour lights gleaming from North Sydney Bay, I look across the channel south to the October beacon lights of Sydney

City. Cast off mooring and throbbing diesel, the mobilize prop forms the swirls of the fluorescent frisky skip. Undercurrent, she sways in reaching the Cabot Strait, entering a calm black night with scary rolls from yesterday's Atlantic storm. The island of islands; I wave your lights goodbye. A lady in the night stands by her car on the ship's deck as I crawl under the back axle, tying the dragging muffler up. She is scared, wondering whether to thank me or not. I dust off, smiling, then like a shadow, I walk off into the night towards the ship's stairway. All that with a spot of tea is goodbye. Here is to U with A toast of tea and Nova Scotia Coat of Arms crest is sewed on the trophy cap.

Yes, I could buy those Jesus boots
Maybe then, pussyfoot my journey across
This ocean blue.

Last leg of journey...
56 miles to go

By Ron Crocker
Telegram Staff Writer

"There were times when I felt like dying . . . and that's the only thing that would have made me give up."

That's a sample of the grit and will power which Monday morning will bring centennial marathon walker Hank Gallant a world's record.

When he reaches St. John's Monday, Gallant will become the first person ever to have completed a coast to coast trek of Canada, on foot and alone.

It was 277 days, 4,180 miles and three pairs of boots ago that Gallant set out from Beacon Hill Park in Victoria, B.C., the western - most tip of the Trans Canada Highway. His destination – Confederation Building, St. John's.

Last night he reached the Moorland Restaurant in Whitbourne, just 56 miles shy of his goal.

During the last nine months, the 24-year-old Tignish, PEI native has been mocked and ridiculed, lauded and lost, arrested and hospitalized. He has slept almost everywhere from his nylon pup tent to jails, Salvation Army homes and grain elevators.

He set out with $280 in cash and a 50 - pound backpack of provisions including tent, sleeping bag, two ground sheets, five pairs white woolen socks, change of clothing, kettle, hunting knife, foot basin, water canteen, vitamin pills, two days of food rationing, two mouth organs and a guitar.

Two miniature flags one bearing the centennial emblem, the other the Canadian maple leaf – flutter on a curved stick two feet above his packsack.

Out of the 277 days on the road so far, he spent about 50 working "to stay alive." Two of his working days were spent in Grand Falls.

He spent four days in a Montreal hospital after being infected with poison ivy and was delayed a day in B.C. with pulled leg ligaments.

Gallant received no help whatsoever from the centennial commission or from centennial committees and in fact his project wasn't even recognized by one committee, back in Prince George, B.C.

"They figured and thought I was some sort of a Moses," he recalled, "and seemed to be expecting me to start walking on water or something." Gallant says he undertook the hike simply as a centennial project..."it was a challenge and I wanted to prove to myself that I could do it."

His performance, he maintains, is modelled after achievements of the famed "Coureur des Bois" of frontier days.

For sentimental reasons and "to capture the coureurs' real feeling and imagination" Gallant camped out for one night on the famous Plains of Abraham and visited the fortress of Quebec.

Six years of preparation and a lifetime of dreaming preceded the hike. His training included six - mile runs every morning before breakfast. His trim five feet, nine inch frame weighed 155 pounds when he set out. Since then he has shed 28 pounds "but I still feel perfect . . . I was carrying extra weight."

He has kept a day to day log of his journey and plans to transform it into a book. "I have plenty of material," he said, "and a few ideas."

When he's not walking, Gallant likes to write and sing folksongs, Bob Dylan style. He claims to have several ready for publication this winter. In British Columbia he worked as a heavy equipment engineer.

Right now he's nearly broke and will have to work in St. John's to finance his trip back.

Canadians generally, Gallant reflected, were very hospitable. "They were particularly friendly in British Columbia and Alberta, Northern Ontario and Quebec, but the best so far has been here in Newfoundland."

Gallant displays a bold "No Rides Please" sign on his back and he has little time for persons who stop to offer him lifts. He even refused to sit in a car for an interview conducted 16 miles west of Whitbourne.

"I don't want anything to do with cars until I've seen that sign by Confederation Building," he said.

He's been averaging 23 miles a day and has three days left to reach St. John's. He won't arrive until Monday morning – his birthday – even if he has to camp for a while outside the city limits.

To kill some time, he'll leave the TCH cross Roach's Line and walk around Conception Bay. Gallant plans to reach the Confederation Building around 11 a.m. and will seek a meeting with Premier J.R. Smallwood before leaving west again.

"I'd like Mr. Smallwood to sign my log book since St. John's marks the end of my journey," he said.

Before straightening his battered flags and bouncing off toward Whitbourne, Gallant calmly announced his next project.

"I'll walk across Europe next year . . . it'll be warmer anyway."

Chapter 17

THE LAST LEG....

My eyes extend in magnitude on this October twelfth salt mist spray morning. We round the Port aux Basques buoy, bringing me in full view of the bald, black, and round rocks of the port and hillsides. An hour passes until finally, I'm stomping on sleep-pricked feet from the deck of Leaf Erixon Ferry; up the dock and around hill road on this Island of my final victory. Three girls wave as they hurry for the 11 A.M. ferry. Funny, reading their pack sign of "drives please", and I, in the opposite form, "no rides please," I hit the road hard down the "new" Trans Canada Highway in Newfoundland.

On a high land swamp, I walk against headwind blow, and the stun spruce shrub is no higher than four feet. Inland North, the rugged Long Range Mountain prism base, has fall leaves that have not withered on sailing winds. On the highway down ribbon shoulder, I view and hear the roar of high foam roll on Cape Ray Cove.

Two-hands sun finds me in A hydro line slash, piling the freshly fallen boughs high to sleep on, away from the swamp moss muck. The sun golds the leaves in this mixed-tinged deciduous forest. I hide by tea fire light away from road-watch-peepers; I never dreamed that this land was so wild, rugged and sounding in beauty. I sleep, smiling, as the motif drone from the Cabot Strait surf spooks the silent fading wink of dusk.

This road marks A walk inland away from the settled Islands outport and across A funnel hill hole that supposedly has blowing winds of 120 M.P.H. that once derailed A freight. Like the dawn, I imagine A forest walk, two days in survey silence among ghost of many Beothuk Indians on the slopes of Anguille Mountains. One hour pass sunset after stuffing a hot beef sandwich, I follow an old moss trail among deciduous trees to A slope view and pitch bedding of A foot or more to keep the back from a cold, wet sponge. While sipping hot tea, I'm afraid of a second winter on the road. Crashing up the trail, snorting charge around bend, I dive for the off-road bushes. I'm wide-eyed gaping on king bull with yards of horn rack; it was probably spooked by A hunter's scent. It's the headhunt chase and trophy bounty season. Rats, my kettle has seen its day, flattened deep in soggy black mud by A split hoof beast, I hit the sack grumbling incoherently. Through the night, I wake with an intrusion among my pin nerve dreams; something furry with cold claw scratchers crawling around my neck collar. I spring up like an elastic, and it scares me out of my wits; A long nose rodent mole.

Morning has A crisp sharpness that wakes my mind when the nose enters early dawn. Breakfast can B offset without McQuacks hot brewed tea. Darn, almost nine months and entering winter's grip.

In the many brooks and rapid rivers flowing from gorge basins among East Long Range Mountains, swims the spawning trout and salmon. Being questioned at A small store where food rations I buy, the generous owner gives me A Newfy camp kettle; this flat wide-round-bottom is tapered to A very small top "seeper". This will B McQuack's second.

"How would U like A shot of screech… me Boy? It'll warm yah up in this weather."

"No thanks, yours is the fourth invite today."

So great the Elysian fields of nature, bouncing and gaping on the highest of high, feeling like A clay model when someday I will return. Then comes the fourth night evening; A Dad with his sons insist on helping me pitch camp, breaking numerous under-boughs on A small hill yards from the highway. Doors are open wide in this land of hospitality. St. Georges on Stephenville Road, I walk these extra miles for A shop to stock up on two days' rations. There's rolling whitehead surf on Bay St. George, and high above, splattered by some seagull pitch, the endless cable muck carriers rotate to the storage dump. A miner's dream.

In the October sixteenth wind, feeling the salt-fresh Gulf through my hair and holding my nostrils sprouting wide, the frozen ground pounds to my singing complacency mind across the Stephenville crossing. School kids on the way home join for A friendly chat after the ice has been broken. Young chap of eight and nine address me, "me boy". Rabbit hunter, with two snared hares of partly turned white fur, meets me on the road.

"How's rabbits?"

"Bad summer, many young died, too wet. Yah, there used to B many back along Brownmoores brook."

We part with A "take her easy, so long buddy."

On black muskeg brook bank under A quarter century growth of fir, I gather my nights mattress. Crow dark, windy clouds with the smell of snow, is blowing down across the Strait of Belle Isle or the bald granite rocks of Labrador, Hudson Bay and maybe the Ice Polar cap. I rush in damp cold dawn, where large flakes like water slush my burden pack, while tying with clasp numb fingers the strings and straps that yells the pain each cold morn. Black Duck Café, I reach on the run; old chap humped with age and rheumatism opens the barred door.

"Come in, out of this dirty morning. I was expecting U last evening, they seen U down the road from Stephenville."

"I slept A mile or less down the road."

"U look froze; I got tea… on and breakfast, we'll have… by the oil heater. Do U like Sugar Pops?"

"Yah!"

"That's our starter."

Inside adjoined store, he rumbles roughly among large delivery carton cases, picks A box, then walks down the hall to another room where he whispers to A hidden person. His third journey later brings A grumbling roar; his wife emerges in house-coat wrap, kicks over an odd carton and hands him the Sugar Pops. "Wifey does the reading and writing, and I… taking care of work."

Wet snow falls till noon and clears up cold; old sol peeps A mid-day warmth on pounding effort along forty miles of mud gravel shoulder. Island Pond and Gallants Hill are in the down-and-up climb of Newfoundland's West coast. Light frost autumn brush portrait of sonnet grayness in age, is nature in its time. Like last night, it washes the hardwood color to whiteness and disappears in drama stage the leaves "adieu" on void moss. Right ankle swells, boots need repair and body cries relief of its perspiring odor, forcing on through darkness quilt to hide my eyes and reach A tub of cleanness. Stumble! Talk to myself, also smile A stupid tired grin to people who come to meet and question me, the Walker. Shoulders slung forward, dangling ape arms on pigeon-toed feet, I receive my first sweet Newfy kiss at three A.M. entering Corner Brook, Newfoundland.

I'm invited to a hotel room where bones of numbness are tossed into A tub of scalding water, numbing thoughts of cold tiredness. Is it A fool they see in me or an adventure they would like to try? Am I proud, thankful to have accomplished this distant walk? Boots are taking the hammering rasp, and I'm sitting too stiff to move, caused by yesterday's forced forty miles. Nervous as butter, a smiling widow reporter interviews me at mid-morning tea. She forgot her film roll, and her motherly smile of pleading kindness has me going through the second walk pose.

Good morning people, you're looking real fine. Merging along the Humber River in A naturally rimmed valley, I'm confined to the black snake highway and speechless silence of West Coast mountains that echo loudly in my face. In A day and A half, with tea breaks and cold hands, I reach Deer Lake.

Only seconds after the lone hoot whistle blows from A midnight freight, my tent flops down, and I crawl from under warmth to A biting night of frost, bare feet. Dollar fifty flashlight follows hip roll stride of the largest black ber…ber..ber… bear I have ever seen. He stayed, but I moved.

I carry ten pounds extra food over long lonesome void-divide to Badger, with pack cutting the shoulders equaling A ton. On Feeder Brook bank, quietness can B felt chilly, as large saucer-shaped snowflakes wet this forest swamp and dancing fire light. Not A whisper from the fish-eating people, the Beothuk Red Indians, who lived in this forest. White man's bounty for A Red Indian was high, and his blood ran in the rivers. When John Cabot discovered Newfoundland, there were five hundred and more Beothuk on this Island; now, we only hear the murmur of the salty biting wind. Time blots their blood on history pages and covers some truth that U may read between the lines.

Twenty-second of October chill, with a light blanket of snow-slush padding the silence, I charge upon A small stream trout and swoop with A large branch, two out of five tail-wigglers. McQuack, steam-whistles A merry hum while seeping china tea. Burning coals under steamy pink trout steak is fit for A king. Birchy Lake narrows, sparkling in mix shadow background of freshly fallen snow; the road is climbing straight, high among the rolling hills of caribou country.

On this sixth "lever du soleil" from Deer Lake, I received a call to have breakfast with highway workmen. I leave later with yesterday's salt pork boiled dinner in lunch-pack under arm, and A good thank you to those highway working boys.

Joe's Lake: Rocky bank points in a tranquil mood, and I sun-warm on rocks while sitting here dangling feet in stinging cold water. I watch in speculation and curiosity the honking wild geese on the shady shore across the way, breaking the nights newly formed ice to reach the wild grass feed in shallow water.

Serene mid-day shadow reaches Badger village, yards before my abiding form. As I skip walk along shadow brook, I imagine reflections of long beard and dancing star-eyed elves in Newfy Swamps. I leave Badger full of moose steaks and roasted spuds, and my shadow is long in four-hands sun. Bill E. of Badger and wifey wave good luck, arousing the village shopkeepers while curtains have peek eyes in upstairs windows. Kids follow to the highway bridge; cheerio, it's been nice having U to dinner. I need not describe the warm tears on cold cheeks, A lump in my throat and feeling silly right down to the grin, singing the beauty of nature. Here on the "Isle of me Boy", hearts are large with a warm welcome. Nineteen gravel shoulder miles to Grand Falls and apple pie is served on road shoulder six miles from town. Such A sweet mother!

Winter! Winter has hurried its process. Late in dark night, I'm inside the Grand Falls town. Where to go with two dollars in pocket? Should have slept in the woods before town, then go looking for two days of grub money job tomorrow. Sitting behind A mahogany desk, A frizzy red hair, crew-cut Corporal glares at the question.

"Do you have a bed for me tonight, Sir?"

"No."

"Even A place to roll out my sleeping bag Sir?"

"It's against our rules. What's your Religion?"

"R.C."

"I'll try the Priest's house."

The tone of voices rings in my ears, "Hello Father, this is Corporal... and we have A little problem... Oh I see, sorry to have bothered U this evening Father". Past mid-night the town falls in subtle sleep. Without money, vagrancy could B A night's cell bunk, but in the drafty hallway, I wait dreaming of a mirage of beds.

Never give up! If adversity presses,

Providence wisely has mingled the cup,

And the best counsel in all your distresses,

is the stout watchword of "Never give up."

Walk each day with sweet words when happy the sun rises bright. Rescued by the Centennial Committee, I'm hushed in tolerance zeal to A gusto hotel room along frost creaking early morning sidewalk. Ohhh! U lucky duck, and I fall asleep standing by the bed.

Old sun peeks through the cracked drawn shades in my room, and I rest my eyes, mind and tired body in the late afternoon. Confusion of ideas and misinformation, I'm disappointed at finding no entertainment stand, so I settle for A board piler job, two days of unloading C.N.R. box cars of rough spruce boards.

Ring around Rosie, U scratch my back, and I'll scratch yours, mostly politics played games. "Hank, U give A good word to the head of government for us?"

"Now sir, I have no political pull but only the pull to carry this pack."

The mischief story of her supposedly dead husband, that is out of town and in her good little heart, invites me to A tasty chicken supper. My great excuse is an early start at morning dawn. Shivering, she stands in the early evening door, waving goodbye.

Outhouse smell on this damp gray October twenty-ninth mid-morn, is similar to the industrial stack refuse following the valley air currents for miles. Bishop's Falls; A father with four sons on Sunday offers me A hot plate of salt pork and cabbage, topped with apple pie. Sitting on a bald black rock in a foot of dried dead leaves, the drops of heavenly rain wets the surroundings and my head as they watch me fill, then part in A thank U shake.

Norris Arm, Newfoundland: A downpour on the green spruce hills streaks the wet on my glasses. The café lady glares at my wet features on the morning spin stool; she fries me two burgers, toast and eggs, tossing it in sliding form down the counter after being asked if I had the money for my meal.

"Could I have the key to the washroom?"

"No, you're too wet and tracking my floor."

Out in the distance, small anchored speck fishing boats look tidy, resting on the calm Exploits Bay water. I wave bye, rounding the viewed bend where the smell and dust is washed by pouring cold rains. On cramped joints moving from highway to lakeshore Indian Arm desolate cabin, I pry A small back window open with a knife. Summer living evacuated, I light the small wood stove warming my chilled bones and dry my clothes. The clatter teeth on bare steel springs and zipped-up sleeping bag……. "Good-night."

Damp large flakes sponge me more than rain; at daybreak departure through the two-foot window on hide-away cabin shore, I'm hungry as hell and twice as cold.

Four French tourists in wet snowy weather stop to converse. My extravagant posture must have shocked them. The conversation is cut short with "let's go to St. Paul's," hee hee hee.

November first; from the Goose-Gander Hotel window in dining room breakfast corner, I watch the early morn descent of an "iron bird" to the International Airport. The clock ticks on center back wall, much like the approaching gray winter clouds as gloomy faces sip warm tea. Very fresh clean skin in dirty clothes after last evening and early morning baths. I have food money for survival and strength to reach my destination, with a complimentary room from Gander Hotel.

Gander Lake, below a new rock bluff cut highway, crane-shovels loads the screaming jenny trucks. Miles, I walk, and all forest has been burnt in eye view from last summer's inferno hell. Noggin Cove's gravel truck driver Bruce highballs his rig to Square Pond Café and returns with a hot chicken sandwich. Warm heart of Newfoundland's hospitality encourages my strides like ripe berries. Rolling, balsam and spruce-covered hills are carved in many statuary forms, and salt inlets bloom with gaze complexion in the early sun morning. Lucky was I for escaping yester-evenings goblins and witches, but treats I could have accepted.

Bona Vista winds blow from North ice polar, tearing my postured awning clothes; one woolen army sweater, rubber rain jacket, T-shirt, blue jeans with worn through knees, tripled patched crotch worn from chafed walking, and four pairs of dirty white wool socks with peeking holes in heels. Pounding steadily through Glover town afternoon and stopping for tea on the bank of Terra Nova River, I'm in the good company of A blue jay and squirrel. I try to feed them, but they raise old hell on the dead snag in back.

Second day with the heavenly mackerel sky darkening to squid juice rain, I walk straight way, fair wind East. I'm drenched with eyes blurred through Terra Nova Park and the high shore bluffs of Clode Sound. The grocery shop in Charlottetown is by the Bay where tiny line cod-boats rest, washed from A day of trawling.

"Spend the night in our room, it's better than out in this rain." Snow-shaking pack on porch steps, the two full-bearded green-shirted geologists return to town for the brew. I soap the suds under A hot shower gurgling drain, choking the frogs on swale pads below.

Factual stories begin at nine near the warm cordial flames from split ash in the fireplace. This actual happening was in a Northern Peninsula outport. Billy, an old cod-oil chap, for five years after N.F.L.D. joined Confederation, received monthly A yellow envelope, A hard card with print stenciled numbers. He ignored "this envelope" with many other mail junk and tossed it into A cupboard drawer until his Torontonian cousin returned to visit in 1958.

"Billy, U must B living well, the fishing and your cheques?"

"Fishing has been poorer and worst each year, and what cheques do U mean? I owe my life to the merchant."

"That yellow envelope U got this morning in the mail, that's your old age pension."

Here was Billy bow-legged, worn-out rheumatism fingers, and A non-reading tycoon of the Herring Inlet, was found. Several thousand dollars; every old maid chasing to marry the wealthy bachelor. Imagine! He was saving them with other paper scraps to plaster his shack walls for insulation. Very coarse and brittle to use those cheques as tissues in the back outhouse.

Like an obedient nag strapped to my burden, I round the bay gorge where the rapids run wild and high-leaps the spawning salmon. Port Blandford looms in darkness, celebrating the English Patriot Guy Fawkes. Kids whoop and dance around the flames, looking like shadows on the witch dog's tail. I sleep in bushes all hung with crystal opal drops, where the haunted dream in a yellow tent stirs me, and I wake and wait for dawn.

Sunday morning, light and coming down rain, I dash for the highway with biting fingers in cold thick Atlantic fog. Burnt spruce calloused feet cries for rest, and forest-lying clouds darken and cling to Shoal Harbour River. All is dying or dead on account of November rains, those charcoal naked deciduous. People I meet in "bonjour" rain are squinting their eyes; I talk but ignore juice sweat running from peak cap among the upside-down clouds. Tall people go and come from church today.

Standing braced and breathing the freshness after the rains, I observe Clareville streets, A carpenter's dream of old Britain. At the Gladney's sunning porch, I watch the sculptured art of a skiff, tacking under A gray sail, bobbing among green silver crested waves. A zephyr salt tip, births the happy song. White speck briny gulls glide gracefully from the ocean's nose, following North West Arm and whiting the capes of Deep bight. The abraded twisted pack frame finally broke in three places; the willow-twig-splice I wrap with shoelaces.

From the quietness of the inland hill, he descends on a mud-waddled footpath; A rabbit-packing old man crossing the highway. Braced, I repair the sagged pack house frame.

"Hello me Boy."

"Hi, sure A wet day; rabbits must B thick by that load!"

"Not really, I snare fifteen miles towards Tug Pond, this is the weekend catch."

Parting in warm handshake, though weather has broken conversation, the hare-man trapper, steadied by walking stick, bow–legged in his seventy-two years of hard work, descends to the village below.

Obey town vertex bluffs peers the unseen like A rolling dream in days greyness. The fog follows low, obscuring everything until the parting sky opens the view of a one-hundred-and-fifty-foot bluff. A day later, November seventh, on a viewpoint that has no scene, the rain film fog screens my lens; seventy-mile wind gusts slap my rain-worn tailcoat. I clutch with stamina and tack the wind against North East blow, following the right-side ditch for shelter. Autumn gales blow on the flat Avalon Peninsula, and I kiss the sheltering forest left behind at Come By Chance. Continuous savage sea roars and the tempest devil surf crashes on rocky reefs and shoals, with only three miles of soil between Trinity and Placentia Bay. Above my view, the torrential mackerel skies with spitting rain and mousey fog, erase the silhouette cape.

Like A rat, cold, wet and crawling, I stumble through a dark swale following the downflow brook. In the shelter of A ten-foot wash bank, with two handfuls of dry bare willows, I stake my tent on rocks in the rain that will not stop. This night of coldness on a bed of stone in "Wolves Gullet", is where the rapids shoot with downpour.

November eighth: Down on A hard chilly riverbed, the northeast blast causes heavy rain showers to stop my daily progress. Throughout the day, I wait for the rain to ease, dozing in damp rest. Inspecting the belching Niagara, I move the soaked tent and bedroll to higher ground from the rising sluice; no dry wood, no tea or warmth of fire.

Before the dingy night vanishes, the tent collapses under six inches of snow, which hinders me from sleep. Cold and damp-stiff, I try bouncing about while packing; there is limited space on A niche frame to balance my pack, taking me ten to fifteen minutes. Crying with nipping smart of frozen tips, the numbed hands tie four strings holding my Gibson solid, then the canvas wrap. Binding is done by teeth, and hands are held swollen and numb for body heat under the sweater. I jolt the pack on shoulders, stumbling slowly along the sound of a rushing stream and around the dark snow-padded gravel bank bend. Up on the highway, I jog down the blacktop East.

Gusty Atlantic winds blow, yet beyond iceberg Arctic pads, the seals flirt in the midnight hour. Getting wet in blinding snow showers while cramps strike the leg with a charley horse, I limp down the road, but the taste of victory is within the heart. Finishing the black bread crust and half of the chocolate keeps me alive with two vitamin pills these past three days. Bleak moorland blueberry shrub is coated wet with whiten snow, and A dozen fluffy scratching gray sparrows are picking the leavings of galloping horses.

Darkness has fallen past, and somewhere stumbling where I don't want to sleep, A rig truck driver, slide-stopping, looks me over; he first thought I was A moose. I count the coppers to four precious dollars for A warm room motel. I scatter clothes over the vents and fall asleep exhausted in A bathtub of hot water.

Snows Pond and Ocean Stream, as I squint eye on this morning of winter's kiss. Stomach full of free breakfast; one pocket, only holding pocket, stuffed with chocolate bars to provide the vigor for twenty-seven miles planned. Name signs roll in richness; Wabana, Brigus, and Topsail. Snow covers both muskeg and burnt bush, also traces of children's footprints that played here months past. People stop, eighteen cars, if toes and fingers run the count, flowing their cup of curiosity to wish me well.

I walk these miles in deep thought before dark along A gravel road and smell the fresh salt mist. Cows crowd under an open-end shed, as I, in moccasin fashion, pad the noise on snow crust field, up the dike and over fences. Beneath the glowing cross, and hill of spruce bush starlight darkness, I stop and listen as farmers check their horses while nostrils snort A frosty vapour steam. The Holyrood village lights are below, and the large cross feels safe, it's above my head.

November sun can kiss your brow through trees on the east slope hill. The tea seeps warm, weak and green as I look out on Conception Bay high above by the marked Holyrood cross. Silver sun gannets drop-fleck on the Atlantic as I dance and sing on frosty snowfields; I may now count those miles ahead.

Three colorful dories with pilot seamen are sculling from stern; there're squids in the cold bite green. Such A view of North Bacon Cove, with hills puncturing brown on whitewashed fields and emerging on A red cliff cape. The dissolving scene is lost and gone in an eclipse of an indigo void. Now the mid-day sun disappears from view behind A rolling white cloud, leaving a lurid glint on the flush countryside.

Being joined in an inquisitive manner by Mr. Marsh at Gullies villa, A hot beef dinner I order, while he drains without A wink, stop or grin, A water glass full of dark rum.

"It's an appetizer, me boy. Here's A rugged life with lots of fun when we play. I fish squid in the bay, selling it for bait to the longliners. You're the boy that's doing this walk, and nearly finished U are. Why don't U celebrate you'll B there tomorrow at St. John's; get drunkly happy me boy."

"Milk will B my drink."

"How do U like our Island?"

"Damn cold, but the people are beautiful and kind."

The old man relates with extended arm about markings of odd occasions.

"It was five years after the great gale, and my story unfolds. I rolled around the bays and outports on converse where I had sailed. I traveled by night U see, where I hid the skiff and covered it, then crossed over the shrubby rock bluff to this Northern inlet village. High on A rock shelf, A quarter mile above town, I pitched A tent ready for the experiment. In the morning sun, I entered with A book and chair, pretending not to notice the many eyes from twelve houses below. Around corners, they peered and pointed. For three days, I remained without any contact with these people, and they… with shy curiosity, would not approach. The third night, as I had come, I went my way. Now from that year's odd happening, they mark certain occasions in conversation; for instance, it was two years after that chap sat up on the hill reading for three days. Others mark by the horrible shipwrecks or destructive storms or the dry year and the big cod."

Newfoundlanders are deep in heart, and news travels fast. Before the crimson sun dips into twilight fields, several homes have opened their pathway gates to join me with tea; the invite of merit soul is always A humble full-course meal. A crippled boy chauffeured by his Dad brings me hot soup, offering me A souvenir gift from his treasured coin collection. "I followed U Hank through most of the walk when news kept U tabbed. Wish I could walk, I'd finish to St. John's with U."

Upper Gullies dance on way to A night at Kelligrews "Soirée", two-party boys on A weekend spree stall their pickup and are convinced that A ride is what I need because the pack is A burden on A Saturday night. "Thanks, I'll make town on foot." Gravel-sprayed choking dust with rubber screeching sound, the tailgate swings as they verbalize their yodeling throats from A bottle of screech.

Darkness falls… tingling from A quilt of jack frost. The squid jigging ground rolls gloomy with the bay buoys moan. On cold frozen top sand below a red shale bank, I roll in round under staked-up tent using boots as a pillow and clatter my teeth on chilly bed rest.

November twelfth: Crawling from under a white frozen tent and meeting glittering sun two hands above bay-slick water, A wave undertow separates the gravel windrow at ebb tide. Mackerel gull on A one leg stand and, with left eye shut, sleeps his morning wait on A few feet from my tent. Driftwood heats tea, sweetened with four lumps of sugar and two blackened cheese sandwiches smoked, I eat the last food rations.

Kelligrews, Newfoundland has stretched its yawn and gone to church in welcoming the ring-bell song. The black wing-tip gulls fly to capelin reef as children skip their Sunday shoes on A frosty lawn. In Foxtrap, having morning tea with Mrs. Grouse, we converse on religion and the generation gap. I found the road through Manuels and Chamberlains, now finally arriving with four hands sun at Café Du

Top Sail. Let's consult the financial situation of the left pocket. Yes, eight greenbacks and thirty-seven cents. "I'll have A hot chicken sandwich with A maple milkshake, thank U."

My affirmative disciplined determination has swayed but never broke; these happy inside tears have burned my eyes with a lump in throat... that makes me dance to join the Trans-Canada Highway East of Paradise. Each step is like A snow fluffy cloud, and many auto-waving spectators follow behind me as I stumble on towards victory.

The red bald top of green rolled hill has eaten its snow topping of the day, and only shadowed darkness lunge my steps. On a conquered hill overlooking the valley squatted lake of lights, cluttering around the bay of briny billows, I enter the hillside bushes. In A small east slope opening where the young four-foot high spruce reflect the heavenly stars and city lights of one mile away, I web thick my last branch bedding in snow which is high on boot laces. I gather dry spruce branches to boil water before carefully measuring quantities of green tea to McQuacks open mouth. Starry nights of passed on dreams are days that have flowed like sweet wine. I pluck my old guitar with nip-pick fingers before A fire that matches the welcome of the city. I can visualize faces in the flames of warmth that smile over the five thousand two hundred and twenty-six miles I have walked. If I could express the words, but I cannot in many ways; for one mile away lies victory.

The wings of black crow they fly, yes... they wake in the morning with loud conks and chirp; my feathered friends. I enter the green world of the squirrel who scampers in carrying away my tossed-out crumbs. The happiest of Birthdays; A lump swallowed throat and tears streak my cheeks. The forest kingdom I embrace with my last farewell wave as the squirrel chatters his measured boundary.

Tossing high on carved out shoulders, the straps and pack is tied with strings and sticks to splint the broken frame. Following a footpath worn by heels of kids who play the games of hide and seek, I walk to the highway and join the cloudy cold east morn, one mile from St. John's limits. Stumbling among clouds on eagle heights, I grin at my odd appearance on this gray fall day. The crotch-bound patched faded jeans, shortened on leg length for use of patching material for the butt, and the gouged-cut hair in hunting knife clip, are A mere reflection of the enduring pack-walk.

I'm welcomed to St John's with happy warm smiles on weekend holiday, and hundreds of skipping laughing children gather along destiny road.

"Hi Hank, I'm Judy. My birthday is today, I'm nine. How old arc U, Hank?"

"Twenty-five, and the happiest year of my life."

It's A week-old stubble and wind-burnt features under A black faded sweat-weathered peak cap as they sing me happy birthday and many centennial songs up the road of happiness. I'm holding the Newfoundland crest, ready to sew the final Coat of Arms above its brim on center ball cap. My nine year old birthday friend leads this amazing chorus of centennial songs. Smiling patrolmen direct the traffic as we swarm the four-lane highway up to Confederation Center.

I, Hank Gallant, am the first walker to cover it all from West to East on the Trans-Canada Highway, the ten provinces. Hoisted and held on shoulders reach, I sign the map of Canada on November 13th at 11 AM… on my 25th birthday.

The world is mine on happy kiss day
The feet that stumbled my reach to keep
Each morning wake A happier beat
Victory victory over defeat.

Signing map of Canada

Miles ending Trans-Canada Highway, St. John's Newfoundland

TRIUMPH.........

These tears of joy in fulfilled dream of stubborn reality. There are few souls that expand the heart on pigeon-toed kiss around this wide Universe. I'm being "echelon" from the warm grasp of those people that show their interest in my victory. The eloquent rhythm of this car, wheeling the speed of thirty MPH with both feet braced on the floor, I'm holding onto the door handle. The quest that lasted two hundred and eighty days, viewing the speed of dated man, leaves me close to the sweet earth and frightened on my first car ride in nine months and one week.

I hide behind a long peak cap and A week-old stubble, and the birthday cake is rolled out to the table window on the bald cliff overlooking St. John's Harbour. "Huzza, huzza...victoire, victoire", but highway dust fills my mind, and it can't penetrate that I'm finished. Blow out in one gust these twenty-five candles on the day I won't forget even when my memory could fail.

It takes all the one hundred and seventeen pounds, burnt with the sun, to crawl into the water tub for a hot soaking. I count six dollars remaining change in my pocket, and I have lost twenty-five pounds. Yelling the echo of my victory that can't imagine that this is the two hundred and eightieth day since the departure of Victoria British Columbia, I skip hop kicking trash cans on A Monday evening pick-up-garbage downtown. The blue jeans smell new, and fifty pennies now remains to celebrate people's noise in the Port Hole of Newfy music.

I christen my toes in the pink Harbour water, just minutes before midnight, alone on a moist-damp creosote plank. I return to my motel room, one beer full, as the light shines through the November winds. "Can the steps proceed further than this cliff and... this Newfoundland rock?"

Made in United States
Troutdale, OR
10/17/2025